"You're Prettier Than I Remembered," He Said.

Annie's face grew warm, and she laughed nervously to cover her embarrassment. "You remember me fat, don't you?"

"I remember..." He touched her cheek, tracing the bone beneath her eye and then the soft hollow below. "I remember that you were beautiful, but not so pretty. I wasn't just being polite when I said you look terrific, Annie. You do."

"Thank you."

"It's complicating things," he warned her.

"What things?" Her voice sounded airy, unable to support itself.

"I didn't come all this way to make a pass at you," Keith murmured, sliding his fingers back past her temple and deep into her hair. "But right now that's exactly what I want to do."

Before she could stop him, he bent and brushed his mouth over hers....

Dear Reader:

Welcome! You hold in your hand a Silhouette Desire—your ticket to a whole new world of reading pleasure.

A Silhouette Desire is a sensuous, contemporary romance about passions, problems and the ultimate power of love. It is about today's woman—intelligent, successful, giving—but it is also the story of a romance between two people who are strong enough to follow their own individual paths, yet strong enough to compromise, as well.

These books are written by, for and about every woman that you are—wife, mother, sister, lover, daughter, career woman. A Silhouette Desire heroine must face the same challenges, achieve the same successes, in her story as you do in your own life.

The Silhouette reader is not afraid to enjoy herself. She knows when to take things seriously and when to indulge in a fantasy world. With six books a month, Silhouette Desire strives to meet her many moods, but each book is always a compelling love story.

Make a commitment to romance—go wild with Silhouette Desire!

Best,

Isabel Swift
Senior Editor & Editorial Coordinator

ARIEL BERK
Together Again

Silhouette Desire

Published by Silhouette Books New York

America's Publisher of Contemporary Romance

SILHOUETTE BOOKS
300 East 42nd St., New York, N.Y. 10017

ISBN: 0-373-05426-2

First Silhouette Books printing May 1988

ARIEL BERK

is not only a novelist, she is also a composer. In her spare time she enjoys activities as disparate as sailing, sunbathing, hiking and visiting museums, but she lets nothing take too much time away from her pleasure in writing.

One

——

"Once upon a time there was a dragon named Sophie. Yes, she was a girl dragon. Have any of you ever seen a girl dragon?"

Annie was greeted with a shrill chorus of "No!" and lots of giggles and snorts.

"Well, most of the time when we think of dragons we think of them as 'he,' not 'she.' But it just so happens that there are lots of she-dragons like Sophie, too. Sophie was a very, very nice dragon. She could do all sorts of neat things: she could jump rope double-dutch—which isn't easy when you've got four legs and a big, long tail—and she could run faster than most he-dragons her size, and she could sing 'The Star-Spangled Banner' without forgetting any of the words, and without her voice cracking when she got to the part about the rocket's red glare, and she could blow smoke through her nostrils in seven different colors. What we're talking about, boys and girls, is one mighty fine she-dragon.

"But Sophie was a very lonely dragon. She was lonely because people were afraid of her. Well, of course people would be afraid of her—wouldn't you be afraid of a dragon?"

Another chorus of "No!" erupted from Annie's rapt young audience.

"Not even one who could blow smoke through her nostrils in seven different colors?"

"No! No!"

Annie grinned. She loved telling stories to children because they knew how to participate in the narrative. They became involved, they became loud, they sprang to their feet and shouted their opinions. They did all sorts of things that grown-ups would never dare.

As a children's librarian, Annie Jameson spent a fair amount of her time sharing stories with youngsters. At the story hours she hosted in the library, she read books to the children. But she wasn't at the library this afternoon, and she wasn't reading. When Tim Shandler had called her earlier that week and asked if she could recommend a professional storyteller to entertain children at Shandler's Department Store during its Family Day promotion, Annie had volunteered herself, free of charge. She liked making up stories, inventing voices for her characters and altering the plot as she went along, based on her audience's response.

This was the third audience she'd faced today, and by far the most enthusiastic. Fifteen children were seated in a semicircle on the carpeted floor before her in a clearing at the center of the store's juvenile department. Behind the children stood a handful of parents. As with Annie's first two storytelling sessions, most of the parents had parked their children in front of Annie and then departed to take care of their shopping.

"So one day Sophie decided to try to make friends with a person," Annie continued. "She honestly believed that if human beings stopped being afraid of dragons and made friends with them, instead, the world would be a much happier place. Not just for dragons, but for human beings.''

Several of the children nodded their heads; they obviously believed that dragons and humans ought to work out their differences. One of the mothers standing at the outer edge of the semicircle nodded, too. Annie noticed that the woman was gently pushing a stroller back and forth as she listened to the story. Inside the stroller an infant lay dozing with a pacifier plugged into its tiny pink mouth. The baby must have been three or four months old. The same age Adam had been...

Annie jerked her gaze away from the peacefully slumbering child. She no longer went into a tailspin whenever she saw a baby. She no longer fell apart. It had been six years since she'd lost Adam. Six years of recovering, rebuilding, learning to enjoy life again. She wasn't going to go into a funk just because she'd happened to glimpse a cute little baby.

"...And Sophie said to the boy, 'I'm a very nice dragon.' But when she said it, all this colorful smoke came pouring out of her nostrils, and the boy was so afraid he ran away.'' Annie was relieved to hear her voice emerging calmly and steadily. She couldn't allow herself to be distracted. On some superficial level, the children sitting on the carpet at her feet needed her—if only to keep them entertained while their parents shopped. They were alive, in the present, and she owed them her full attention.

She continued weaving her tale, describing the colors of smoke that at first frightened all the people but gradually won them over. The smoke was so beautiful, Annie explained, that the people couldn't resist it. Their admiration for Sophie's smoke helped the human beings overcome their fear of dragons. They made friends with Sophie, and everyone lived happily ever after.

Life didn't always work out that well, but Annie wasn't going to disillusion the children. Let them think that dragons were magical. Let them think that within even the deepest fear and pain, one could sometimes see a rainbow in the smoke. On good days, like this cloudless autumn Saturday, Annie almost believe it herself.

Inspired by the example set by a couple of parents, the children clapped their hands and hollered thank-yous. At least three children had the audacity to demand another story. Annie smiled and shoved back a few blond wisps of hair that had unraveled from her braid and fallen across her lightly freckled cheeks. "Maybe you guys don't need a break, but I do," she said apologetically. "Let me get a drink of water and then I'll tell you another story, okay?"

She stood and stretched. The wooden stool the store had provided for her wasn't very comfortable, and after three half-hour story sessions her back was beginning to stiffen. She dug the heels of her palms into the small of her back and rolled her head from shoulder to shoulder to loosen the muscles in her neck. Then she started toward the cashier's counter where a pitcher of ice water was waiting for her. And froze in place when she saw Adam's eyes.

No, not Adam's. The dark, down-sloping eyes that captured hers didn't belong to a child. Their shape resembled Adam's, with the heavy fringes of lash, and the irises so deep a gray as to appear black...but Adam's eyes had been full of innocence and unquestioning love. These eyes were weary and old. They were eyes that had seen too much smoke and not enough rainbows.

There was only one person in the entire world who had eyes like those. If Adam had lived there would have been two people: father and son.

Keith LaMotte took a step toward Annie, circumventing the cluster of children swarming around her. She tore her gaze away from his eyes and found herself staring instead at his lips—firm, thin lips that appeared incapable of smiling—and then at his chin, square and rugged. Her fingers knew the shape well; countless times they had traced the harsh angle of his jaw, drawing his mouth to hers.

"Hey, lady, why don't you get your water so's you can tell us another story?" a small boy yelled up at her.

She inhaled. She hadn't realized she'd been holding her breath, but when her lungs filled with oxygen she felt a rush of sensation, as if she were waking from a bad dream. Unable to trust her voice, she nodded in the boy's direction and edged away from the crowd. For some reason, she thought that if she could slip behind the rack of children's snowsuits to her left, she could avoid Keith.

Stupid thought. As soon as she made her move, he darted behind the rack as well. They nearly collided, and he curled his fingers around her upper arm to keep her from stumbling.

"I'm sorry," he said.

For a long moment she simply gaped at the spot where his hand curved around her arm. She wasn't sure whether he was holding her up or holding her in place, whether if he let go of her she'd fall or run away. She studied the suntanned length of his fingers, which contrasted vividly with the pale blue of her sweater. He had never worn a ring, she remembered, wishing she didn't feel so dazed, wishing her brain would focus on something more substantial than her utterly irrelevant memory of the ring she'd bought for him and he'd refused to wear. He used to claim that, though he thought the ring was nice, he didn't like wearing jewelry; it made his fingers feel clumsy. She wondered what had become of the ring, whether he'd given it away or thrown it away, whether it was still wedged inside the velvet box in which it had come.

"I went to the library this morning, just before noon," he explained. "They were about to close up, but one of the librarians told me I'd find you here this afternoon. I'm sorry, Annie. I didn't mean to shock you.''

"Well, you did," she declared, lifting her face to his.

Their gazes locked. If only his eyes didn't remind her so much of Adam's...as if Keith would ever remind her of anything but the child they'd had together, the child they'd lost.

"You look terrible," she blurted out. It was true. His high brow was marked with worry lines, as was the skin at the outer corners of his eyes. His dark brown hair was too long to be stylish, and a few strands of premature gray threaded through the thick waves. Annie fleetingly wondered whether she had aged as much as Keith had in the past six years.

The crow's-feet framing his eyes deepened, and she realized that he was smiling—a strange, crooked smile that lacked the dimples she had always been a sucker for. "You're looking terrific yourself, Annie," he murmured.

"What are you doing here?" she asked, finally beginning to think rationally. She noticed the new, brightly colored snowsuits to her right, and to her left a stack of shelves filled with underwear patterned with Smurfs and super heroes. She was in Shandler's, a small department store in Brenton, Connecticut—three thousand miles from California, from the sun-blessed rural community in the Sacramento Valley where she and Keith had set up house and, for one brief, idyllic year and a half, had been a family.

"What do you think I'm doing here?" Keith returned, his smile becoming wistful. "I wanted to find out how Sophie the dragon was making out."

"I need a drink," Annie mumbled. Her knees felt wobbly beneath her, and her desire for water had less to do with the wear and tear her throat had endured in the story sessions than with her genuine fear of passing out.

"It's a little early for me," Keith said, misunderstanding her, "but if you want, sure, we'll get a drink. You're the local, you must know where the nearest bar is."

"I meant water," she corrected him. Her gaze dropped to his hand on her arm again. If he let go of her, she would be able to walk over to the cashier's counter and get a drink. But if he continued to hold her, if he held her long enough, maybe she'd remember what it used to feel like being held by him.

It was too many years ago; too much had happened since then. No matter how long his hand remained on her, she would never let herself remember.

"Annie." His voice was low, husky, oddly seductive. "I've spent the past three years looking for you." His gaze shifted to her arm, too. Slowly, reluctantly, he relaxed his fingers, and his hand fell from her. "When will you be done with your story sessions?"

When? As if there were any way she could fulfill her storytelling obligations now. As if she could sip some water, dance back to her stool and regale a fresh group of children with an amusing yarn about another wayward dragon, or a confused duck or a little boy with a magic molar that made all his food taste like chocolate. As if she could continue living her life as though everything were normal.

Keith was here. For the first time since he'd walked out of her life six years ago, Keith was standing before her, speaking to her, invading the cozy universe she'd constructed for herself in his absence. She couldn't go back to telling stories.

"I . . . uh . . . I'd better talk to Tim Shandler," she stammered, moving her arm as if to make certain it still worked after Keith had touched it. "I think he was expecting me to stay till four, but . . ." She ran out of words, out of energy. She prayed for the strength to get herself across the store to Tim Shandler's office.

Taking a step, she felt a violent trembling in her knees. Good lord, she might just faint, after all.

Keith clamped his hand around her arm again, sure and solid. This time she was forced to admit that he was holding her up. He'd kept her from collapsing once before, one ghastly morning when she'd gone into the nursery to wake Adam. Keith had kept her from collapsing that morning, supported her, refused to let her fall. Here he was, once again, refusing to let her fall.

"Where are we going?" he whispered, bowing slightly so that his lips were next to her ear. "Over there, to that stockroom area?" He slid his hand down to her elbow to be less obvious about the fact that he was holding her up. Then he escorted her through the clothing displays, past the mannequins that were scantily draped with ladies' lingerie, past the curtained fitting rooms and glass showcases filled with leather wallets and costume jewelry, and through a door into a back hallway lined with metal shelves filled with inventory.

Keith halted at the first open door, which led into a cramped office. Tim Shandler, the balding middle-aged owner of Shandler's Department Store, stood behind a cluttered metal desk, with a telephone receiver pressed to his ear. As soon as he spotted Annie in the doorway, with Keith behind her, he held up his index finger and turned away. "Listen, Max—I'll call you back," he said into the phone. "The place is hopping with this Family Day promotion. But get the damned belts shipped in by next week, all right?" He hung up, then turned back to Annie. "How's the storytelling going?" he asked. "Word around the store is, the kids are eating it up."

"I'm..." Annie's voice cracked, and she leaned backward as her energy faltered. Her shoulders came in contact with the upper portion of Keith's chest. Through the wool of his crewneck sweater, through the cotton of the shirt he had on underneath it, she discerned the lean muscles of his torso, the hard, streamlined shape of his athletic body. His face had aged, his hair was beginning to turn gray, but his body was as sleek and powerful as she'd remembered it.

No. She didn't remember. He'd left, and she had deliberately made herself numb. She wouldn't remember how good it had been with Keith.

She swallowed, then forced herself to speak. "I'm afraid I've got to—"

"Are you all right?" Tim broke in, charging around the desk and shooting an alarmed look at Keith. "You're as white as a sheet, Annie. Come here, come here and sit down." He grabbed her hands and led her into the office, to a folding chair near the desk. She was grateful to him for pulling her away from Keith. Sort of grateful, she amended. She'd felt less shaky leaning against him than she felt sitting on yet another hard, uncomfortable chair.

Tim was trying to push her head down between her knees. "Breathe deep, honey. You look like you're going to keel over."

"I'm not," she insisted, her voice muffled by the thick denim of her jeans as her mouth collided with her knee.

"What's going on?" Tim asked. Judging from the sound of his voice, he had directed the question not to Annie but to Keith. "Who the hell are you?"

"I'm...her ex-husband," Keith said.

"He is not!" Annie swung her head up so quickly that, for a moment, the blood rushed out of it and she very nearly did keel over. She gripped the edge of the desk until her vision cleared. "He's not my ex-husband," she said in a low, fierce voice. "He's an old...acquaintance, and—" She clamped her mouth shut. She didn't owe Tim Shandler any explanations.

"I'm afraid she's in no condition to tell the children any more stories today," Keith said, his tone as even as hers was frantic. "I'd like to take her home."

Tim eyed Annie quizzically. "What do you want, Annie? Do you want me to get rid of this guy?"

"No," she said. Keith's presence rattled her, but she wasn't about to let Tim kick him out into the street.

Tim favored Keith with a dubious scowl. "This is a small town, buddy, and we all know each other here. We look out for each other. Now, if you've come to make trouble for Annie—"

"I swear I haven't," Keith said earnestly.

"It's all right, Tim," she said, pushing the stray hairs back from her face again. "I'm okay. But... he's right. I won't be able to do any more stories today."

"Of course not, honey. Of course not." Tim clasped her hands and helped her to her feet. "Do you really want to leave with this guy?"

She nodded weakly. "I'll be all right, Tim."

"Well. Thanks for helping out here. Are you sure I can't pay you for—"

"It was my pleasure, Tim. Really." She saw Keith reaching for her elbow. The sight seemed to cause her adrenaline level to rise, because she suddenly found herself fully capable of marching to the office door and out. It was a defensive move, a self-protective act. She would do anything to keep Keith from touching her again.

Apparently he understood that she didn't want his assistance. He trailed her as she walked briskly through the store. Near the front door, a frazzled father, with a lollipop-sucking toddler perched on one arm, stopped Annie and asked, "Excuse me—when is the next story session going to start?"

She felt a pang of guilt about stranding Tim Shandler without anyone to amuse the children of his customers, and another, stronger pang of guilt about stranding the children themselves. She had thought that, when it came to children, she had used up her lifetime supply of guilt long ago. Perhaps guilt was a renewable resource.

Or perhaps Keith had brought a fresh supply along with him. All of a sudden, Annie felt guilty for everything: for having brought a baby into the world and having lost it, for reneging on her promise to tell children stories all afternoon at Shandler's. For hating Keith, *hating* him.

The midafternoon sun slammed down onto Main Street and the Brenton town green, causing Annie's eyes to sting. She couldn't stand the clear, crisp blue of the sky. The leaves on the maple, sycamore and oak trees lining the green were ablaze with autumn hues; the vibrant color seemed to burn her corneas.

"Where should we go?" Keith asked, his voice drifting down to her from his superior height. "Where can we talk?"

"We have nothing to talk about," Annie argued, refusing to turn to him.

Keith chose to ignore her assertion. "What's that place over there, Riley's? I think I could use a drink, after all."

Exhaling, Annie pursed her lips, dug her hands into the pockets of her jeans and started down the sidewalk to Riley's. She'd never been inside the bar before; it always looked dark and uninviting to her. But then, Annie wasn't much of a drinker, nor was she particularly interested in meeting men. What other reasons were there for a single woman to patronize a bar?

Riley's was probably a safe place to take Keith. If they sat outdoors on the green and talked, they might be seen by people she knew, and then she'd be forced to make introductions and answer questions. And taking Keith to Riley's seemed far preferable to taking him home with her.

The bar was gloomy; the paneled walls of the vestibule were decorated with a few bedraggled paper shamrocks left over from St. Patrick's Day. The bar's interior was also paneled and poorly lit. A massive bar consumed the front half of the long room; beyond it were several booths and tables. A few men sat at the bar watching a baseball game on the television set, but the tables were empty.

The men all turned at Annie's entrance, their eyes bright with fascination. Keith placed his hand possessively on her shoulder and steered her past the bar to one of the booths. She grudgingly appreciated the gesture. She was in no mood to parry any pickup attempts.

Almost as soon as they were seated in the shadowy booth, a waitress materialized and asked for their orders. Annie requested a club soda, Keith a beer. The waitress nodded and vanished.

Gradually Annie's eyes adjusted to the dim light. She stared across the table at Keith, concentrating on his physical presence to avoid being crowded by memories. He was still an extremely attractive man, even if he did look terrible. The crow's-feet and silver hairs somehow made his face more interesting than it had been six years ago. Then, he'd been gorgeous; now, he still looked gorgeous, only he looked more three-dimensional, more complex. Which, Annie supposed, he was.

His sweater appeared expensive, a soft aquamarine wool that hugged his lean torso. His wristwatch, a thin gold wafer with a matching gold band, appeared expensive, too. His legs were hidden by the table, but when Annie and Keith had walked across the green she'd noticed that his tailored corduroy slacks fit him well, enhancing his long legs and trim hips. He'd kept his body in excellent shape.

She wondered what he'd been doing for the past six years. She despised herself for wondering.

While she studied him, he studied her, and when she wasn't wondering about him she wondered about what he was thinking as he looked at her. She wondered whether her eyes still reminded him of polished turquoise stones, as he used to claim they did, and whether he was surprised to find her thin. When he'd left, she had been carrying around an extra fifteen pounds of weight, an unwelcome souvenir of her pregnancy. Her chin and cheeks had been less clearly defined, her waist at least two inches larger, her hips wider.

Now she had the same measurements she'd had when Keith had first met her. Yet she knew she'd aged, too. She might still wear her hair long, woven into a braid down her back, and she might still forgo cosmetics for a fresh-scrubbed look. But there was no way time and heartache would have failed to leave their marks on her.

"How did you find me?" she asked, amazed and pleased by her sedate tone. She didn't yet have the courage to ask *why* he had found her. She thought it best to start simple.

He spotted the waitress approaching with their drinks, and he waited until they'd been served before giving his answer. "It wasn't easy," he noted. "Obviously you didn't want to be found. At least not by me."

"But you found me anyway." She pulled the lime wedge from the rim of her glass and placed it, unused, on her paper coaster. Then she took a long sip of the cold, fizzy drink. It soothed her raw throat, but it didn't do much to soothe her raw nerves. "Teri didn't tell you where I was, did she? If she did, I'll—"

"No," Keith said, cutting Annie off. He tasted his beer, then lowered the glass mug to the table with a heavy thud. "I all but tortured your sister, but I couldn't get her to break. At least she didn't hang up on me. Your parents did."

Annie nodded. Her parents had never liked Keith. More accurately, they had never *let* themselves like him. If they'd given him a chance, they would have found him a personable young man, well educated, with a degree from a prestigious law school. But they'd never accepted the fact that he and their daughter had established a home without the benefit of marriage, that they'd moved in together and exchanged rings—Annie had worn hers even though Keith had never worn his—and had a baby without legal sanction. "If he really loved you, he would marry you," Annie's mother used to declare, refusing to acknowledge that the lack of an official wedding certificate was as much Annie's choice as Keith's.

They had both been idealistic back then. They'd believed that the most important thing was their love, that they didn't need what they disdainfully called "the piece of paper"—that "the piece of paper" would, in fact, taint their love and devalue it. After Keith left, Annie often found herself contemplating whether "the piece of paper" might have held them together through their crisis. She had always concluded that a relationship held together by nothing but a piece of paper wasn't a relationship worth keeping.

Annie's sister, Teri, had been much more accepting of Keith. Sometimes, only partially in jest, she used to call him "brother." But after he'd left, Annie's first way station had been Teri's apartment in Portland. Teri had been the one to witness Annie's unhappiness, and she'd sworn then that she would never forgive Keith for walking out on her sister.

"Teri talked to you?" Annie asked.

Keith nodded. "I hounded her for weeks. I even went to Oregon to confront her, face-to-face. She wouldn't tell me anything—except that you were doing well and I should leave you alone."

Annie wondered why Teri had never mentioned Keith's visit to her. For an instant, she was angry with her sister for having kept such a secret from her, and then she forgave Teri. Teri probably hadn't said anything because she didn't want to upset Annie.

Knowing in advance that Keith was looking for her might have upset Annie, but it wouldn't have upset her as much as having him pop up unexpectedly in Shandler's on a glorious October afternoon. "So, how did you find me?" she repeated, her delivery impassive even though her mind was spinning.

"Not through your family, not through your friends." He took another drink, then shoved the mug to one side and rested his elbows on the table, propping his head in his hands. "I contacted Meryl, Cindy, Darla Kaminer—she's married, by the way. Darla Roth now. She said she hadn't heard from you since you left your sister's place. None of them had."

"I..." Annie sighed. "I cut a lot of ties when I came east."

Keith nodded. Something in his eyes lit up, something in those profoundly dark irises glimmered with recognition and understanding. Annie comprehended that he, too, had cut a lot of ties in the past few years. "I finally tracked you down through the career office at UC-Berkely."

"What?"

"It was a long shot. I asked them where they'd sent your school records. I figured that if you'd applied for a job somewhere, you might have asked the school to send along your file with your grades and letters of reference. They told me you had requested that they forward your records to the University of Connecticut."

"They told you that?" Annie cried indignantly, furious that her alma mater would have divulged such personal information. "That's unethical."

"It is," Keith agreed. "I bribed one of the clerks to get her to help me."

"Bribed? You paid a bribe?" Annie's indignation waned enough to sense the compliment in his actions. She couldn't imagine Keith wanting to locate her so badly that he'd bribe people. "How much?" she asked, grinning shyly.

His answering smile was bittersweet. "Enough. Too much." His gaze drifted past her to focus on the grain of the wood paneling on the wall. "I would have gladly paid ten times as much," he confessed in a near whisper.

Why? Why had he been so anxious to find her? Once again she considered asking him that essential question; once again she chickened out. "Did you bribe someone at UConn, too?" she asked instead.

"No. I conned them." He drank some beer, set down the mug and drummed his fingers nervously against the table-top. "You had majored in English at Berkely, so I thought maybe you'd gone on for a Ph.D. I called up the graduate office and told them I was the personnel director of some fictitious company and I'd received a résumé from one Anne H. Jameson claiming to have a Ph.D. in English from UConn. I wanted the year confirmed."

Anne *H.* Jameson? Annie's middle name was Catherine. Had Keith forgotten? She hadn't forgotten his middle name—David—or his birthday—June first—or his passion for bakery-fresh rye bread and his virulent hatred of raisins.... She cursed silently. Where had all this trivia arisen from? How could she have remembered such nonsense?

"The ploy worked," he continued. "They checked their records and said, 'No one named Anne *H.* Jameson has gotten a graduate degree here, but we do have an Anne *C.* Jameson who got an MLS here three years ago.' I didn't even know that an MLS was a master of library science—"

"I don't understand," Annie interrupted. "Why did you ask for Anne *H.* Jameson?"

Keith's eyes narrowed on her. Again she detected a glimmer in them, something tender and empathetic, something suggesting both sadness and affection. "I didn't know what I was asking for, Annie," he explained. "If I'd given them your real name, they might have thought you were a liar, misrepresenting yourself. I didn't want to do anything that would hurt you."

She smothered the urge to scream. He didn't want to hurt her—was that a fact? Then why had he left her? Why had he disappeared when she needed him so much?

That was an unproductive line of thought, and she quickly dismissed it. She inhaled deeply to calm down and did her best to convince herself that the pain Keith had inflicted so long ago no longer hurt her, that she'd recuperated thoroughly and didn't really hate him anymore. Wasn't that what the past six years were all about—getting over it, getting over him and moving on?

"So," she said lightly, addressing her club soda more than Keith. "So you found out I had a master's degree in library science. Then what?"

"I got in touch with the American Library Association. You're a member and you're on their mailing list. They told me you have your journals sent to the Brenton Town Library." He lifted his mug in a silent toast, whether to Annie or to himself, she wasn't sure, and downed the remaining beer. His eyes lingered on her as he swallowed and placed the mug on his coaster.

He seemed to be waiting for a reaction from Annie, and she endeavored to give him an unemotional one. "That's an awful lot of sleuthing," she summed up. "Sherlock Holmes couldn't have done better."

"Do you like being a librarian?" he asked.

She felt her patience fraying. Surely Keith hadn't gone to so much trouble just to ask her how satisfied she was with her career. But she contained her agitation as best she could. "I'm a children's librarian, and yes, I like it. I'm very happy with my job, and with Brenton." *And without you,* she almost added.

He seemed acutely aware of her sentiments. He nodded again, his eyes losing what little sparkle they'd had, and raked his fingers through the long, dense thatch of hair drooping down onto his brow. "I had to see you, Annie," he murmured, his voice low and intense. "I'm sorry, but I had to. I don't mean to open old wounds, and I don't mean to turn your world upside down. But . . . I had to see you."

"Why?" Out of bravery or sheer recklessness, she asked the question she'd been afraid to ask, the only real question there was. "Why are you here?"

He studied her from across the table. His vision absorbed the girlish style of her hair, the triangular shape of her head—broad enough from temple to temple to accommodate her wide-set blue eyes, tapering along hollow cheeks to her sharp, fragile chin. He perused the slender length of her neck, the narrowness of her shoulders, and what was visible of her slim, fine-boned figure. And he took in the pallor of her skin, the graceful ridges of her knuckles as she rested her hands on the table, the fullness of her lower lip, which she'd tried, with varying success, to keep from trembling ever since he had invaded her story session, invaded her world.

He studied her, this woman he'd been so close to, and realized that she was a stranger to him. A stranger and a lover, both.

He'd known the answer to her question when he'd requested a sabbatical from work, passed his two pending cases along to one of his colleagues at the office, packed a bag and boarded a plane out of Los Angeles. He'd known the answer when he'd disembarked in Hartford, picked up his rental car and followed the map south and east to the exurban village of Brenton. He'd known the answer last night, when he'd checked into the motel on the outskirts of town, when he'd unpacked, climbed into bed, turned off the light and stared for hours at the ceiling, blaming his insomnia on jet lag and discordant time zones and nothing else. He'd known the answer that morning when he'd consumed a light breakfast in the motel's coffee shop, and when he'd cruised around Brenton, trying to get a sense of the town, and when, at a few minutes before noon, he'd scaled the pompously expansive concrete steps leading up to the entrance of the library, discovered that twelve o'clock was closing time on Saturdays and that Annie had already left the library to participate in a department store's Family Day promotion.

But the instant he'd seen her, the instant his eyes had met hers across a sea of rambunctious children ... he'd known he had to see her. But he no longer knew why.

In fact, as he gazed at her through the bar's gloom, he began to question whether he knew anything at all.

Except that he had to be here. Except that he'd done the right thing in coming.

Two

"When are you leaving?" she asked.

As soon as she spoke the words, she realized how tactless she sounded. But she felt that it was safe to assume that Keith had no intention of taking up residence in Brenton. Had he come just for the afternoon, or for the month? Where was his home? What was he planning?

For heaven's sake, he couldn't even tell her why he'd come. When she'd finally found the nerve to ask him, all he'd said was, "I don't know, Annie. I don't know." She had to be crazy to think he'd be able to tell her how long he intended to stay.

Wisely, he didn't bother answering her question directly. "I've got a room at the Brenton Motor Inn," he informed her. "Could we have dinner together tonight?"

A small laugh escaped from her. She could count on the fingers of one hand the number of dinner dates she'd been on since moving to Brenton—not through any fault of her own but because Brenton simply wasn't the sort of place that attracted singles of either sex. It was a family community, surrounded by commercial orchards and untamed forests, boasting not a single condominium or apartment complex within its borders.

A few unattached men lived in Brenton, and Annie was pretty sure she knew them all. She'd spent a few evenings with Steve Harper, a widowed father of three who owned Brenton Books and Stationery on the green, and they'd gotten along well. But the chemistry hadn't been right. Neither she nor Steve had felt much of a thrill when they'd kissed, so they'd chosen not to risk their friendship by pushing the romance. She had also gone out twice with Ronnie Williamson, who was divorced and deserved to be, or so Annie deduced after two dreadful evenings with him. And one long-ago Saturday night she'd engaged in an unpleasant wrestling match with Stanley Warwick, who had sworn to Annie he was divorced but who, it turned out, was only separated from his wife, with a reconciliation in the works.

Brenton's all-but-nonexistent social scene suited Annie well enough. She wasn't averse to finding male companionship, but if it never happened, if she was doomed never to experience a settled, secure domesticity with someone, at least she'd experienced something like it once.

Living with a man she loved had been wonderful—but it had also, ultimately, been devastating. After Keith had left, Annie had been hard-pressed to remember the wonderful parts of their relationship: the joy of making a commitment, the intensity and exclusivity of it, the comfort of knowing that Keith was hers and she was his and that "home" and "together" were interchangeable terms, the ecstasy of being totally, all-consumingly in love.

They had known each other for over a year before they'd made that commitment. When they'd met, Annie had been a senior at Berkeley and Keith had been in his final year of law school. Their first dates had been casual, as college dates so often were—a pizza here, a party there, cups of espresso drunk on a café patio under a starry sky, long-winded debates about the Meaning of Life. And somewhere, somehow, their love had flourished, evolved, grown too immense to ignore.

Although Keith was about to become a lawyer, he professed little desire to make scads of money writing contracts or negotiating divorces. He wanted to become involved in public interest law, he told Annie, and he wanted to live in a small town, one that was unpolluted and uncorrupted. Annie had grown up in Portland, gone to school just outside San Francisco and dreamed of living in a small town, too. So, after they'd both graduated, they packed up their belongings and moved to Orland, a speck of a farming hamlet near the college town of Chico in California's North Central Valley. Keith took a job assisting a lawyer who represented migrant farmworkers in the region, and Annie held a job clerking in a bookstore near Chico State University—until she became pregnant.

They hadn't planned Annie's pregnancy, but they were thrilled by it—Annie was, anyway. She was probably too young to become a mother, emotionally if not physically. And she and Keith didn't have much money. But living costs were ridiculously low in Orland, and the prospect of having a baby elated her. As far as getting married, who needed it? Not Annie, not Keith. They didn't require the state's blessing for what already existed in their hearts.

Keith had been happy about Annie's pregnancy, too, although he never seemed quite as enthusiastic as she was. Annie supposed that it was hard for him to be—after all, everything was happening to her, inside her body, not his. She was the one who nourished the fetus, who felt it moving within her. She was the mother, and the baby was a part of her. Keith was an outsider, an observer, and no matter how pleased he was about becoming a father, he would always be one step removed.

That was how Annie had analyzed it, anyway. That was how she justified his reaction to Adam's death. He had been sad, but she'd been grief-stricken. He had been able to walk away from it, but to this day she still carried the pain inside her.

He'd walked away and now, all of a sudden, he'd walked back. And asked her to have dinner with him. "Look, Keith," she said, hoping she didn't sound too short-tempered. "You must be very proud of yourself for having found me after so much effort, but I'm not really in the mood to celebrate your success. This reunion was your idea, not mine."

"I know," he agreed. "I'm sure you're furious with me—"

"No," she insisted, gazing sincerely at him. What she felt for him wasn't hate, but rather a shadow of the emotion, a small echo of it. She *had* hated him. She'd hated him as recently as a half hour ago. But she didn't hate him anymore.

"Then have dinner with me," he requested.

She sighed and looked away. Why should she have to sacrifice her evening so that Keith could work out whatever demons had motivated him to come here?

At her hesitation he cursed. "I'm so presumptuous," he chastised himself. "You already have plans for tonight, don't you."

Annie's eyes swung back to his. "No, I don't." The words slipped out.

"Why not?" he asked.

The question wasn't posed in a critical way. Keith seemed genuinely curious about why Annie didn't have a date lined up for Saturday night.

She laughed. "Keith, what would you have done if you'd come all this way and discovered I was married?"

"I had no expectations either way," he claimed. "Even if you were married, Annie, we would still need some time together. We need a chance to straighten out our past. I do, anyway."

"It was so long ago," Annie argued gently. "Can't we just let it be?"

"Maybe you can. I can't. At least I haven't been able to yet." Keith reached across the table and folded his large hand around her smaller one. "Have dinner with me tonight, Annie. Please."

She laughed again, a hushed, nervous sound, barely audible over the racket coming from the television set above the bar. "Brenton closes down early on Saturday nights," she warned him. "I don't know where you live these days, Keith, but if you're looking for a gourmet feast, you're not going to find it here."

"Then we'll drive somewhere else. I rented a car. We can go wherever you want."

Annie meditated. She knew of a few nice restaurants in Meriden. It had been a long while since she'd last eaten out. And, loath as she was to admit it, she did want to talk more with Keith. She wanted to learn what he'd been up to all these years, where he'd been and how he'd been. She wanted to learn what it was that had compelled him to set out in search of her.

"All right," she accepted. "We'll have dinner. You can pick me up—or better yet, I'll pick you up. I know where the Brenton Motor Inn is." For some reason, she wasn't ready to let Keith see where she lived. His sudden intrusion into her world was jarring enough. She wanted to keep her home safe from him.

Keith seemed on the verge of debating with her, but he stifled himself. Undoubtedly, he knew that it he quibbled over the mechanics of who picked up whom, she'd likely back out on him altogether. "Would seven o'clock be all right?" he asked.

"Seven o'clock. Sure."

He offered Annie a brief smile, then released her hand, dug into his hip pocket and pulled out his wallet. After leaving several bills on the table, he slid out of the booth and helped Annie to her feet.

She hadn't wanted his assistance in Shandler's, but she'd needed it. Now she no longer needed it. Her knees no longer felt gelatinous, her head no longer light and dizzy. She was totally capable of standing by herself.

Perhaps that was why his courtesy didn't rankle as it had at the store. Perhaps that was why now she felt an unexpected warmth spread through her at his quiet, certain touch.

Neither of them spoke as they left the bar and strolled across the green. Outside Shandler's, Annie told Keith that her car was parked in a lot behind the store, and then she took her leave of him. He watched from the sidewalk as she strolled down the narrow alley between Shandler's and the shop next to it, her braid of corn-colored hair swaying between her shoulder blades, her slim denim-clad legs carrying her in purposeful strides until she vanished from view.

She was pretty. He had remembered her as beautiful, but not so specifically pretty. Age had added an elegance to her youthful face, an alluring hollowness to her cheeks. Her eyes, he recalled, used to bring to mind turquoise stones, but they didn't anymore. Turquoise was opaque. Annie's eyes were translucent, sparkling with facets of light like precisely cut gemstones. And her body, so slender, so magnificently proportioned, so graceful...

She had always been the stronger one, he mused as he turned away and headed toward the rented Pontiac, which he'd parked near the library. Annie had been the stronger one when Adam had died, and in many ways she was still stronger than Keith. The fact that she'd become ashen at the sight of him, that she'd become shaky and breathless, didn't mean she was weak. It only meant that she was shocked—a reasonable reaction under the circumstances.

She had been pale and shaken the morning she'd found Adam, too. On the surface, Annie had been the frail one, Keith the sturdy one, on top of things, in control. But Adam's death had been a shock, too—the worst shock imaginable.

In some cases, with the syndrome there were warning signs: a congenital predisposition, something to make parents extra vigilant. In some cases, infants could be strapped to machines that signaled the parents if there was an interruption in the infants' breathing patterns. A few years after Adam's death, Keith had finally found the fortitude to do some research on Sudden Infant Death Syndrome, to learn whatever he could about the capricious condition that had snatched his son away.

His son. It had taken Keith a long time before he allowed himself to think of Adam as his baby. *His* baby. *His* son.

He had never questioned his paternity, nothing like that. He and Annie had been in love and they'd been faithful. Adam had looked like Keith. Annie used to go on about how father and son were practically identical. Keith hadn't thought they were—Adam, after all, had been tiny and baldish, with ruddy skin, a little pug nose, a sliver of neck beneath his double chin and pudgy, pinchable cheeks. But Keith had never denied that there was a resemblance between him and the baby—especially in their eyes.

Even though he'd been a proud father, he had tended to think of Adam as Annie's baby. She'd been the one at home with Adam, raising him, nursing and nurturing him. Annie and Adam had been a tight team, inseparable, constantly communicating with each other in alien coos and gibberish syllables. Keith had never been quite sure how he was supposed to fit in.

The morning Adam died Keith fit in by taking over. He heard Annie's scream, rolled out of bed and raced to the nursery. As soon as he entered, he experienced a sense of distance, of control. All of a sudden he had a purpose: to take care of everything.

Keith still remembered the way Adam felt when he pulled the baby from Annie's arms and laid him back in the crib. And the way Annie felt when he led her from the nursery, his hand tight around her arm to keep her from collapsing. He sat her on a kitchen chair, handed her a glass of water and then telephoned the police. He spoke calmly and precisely, first to the police dispatcher and then to Adam's pediatrician. All the while, Annie sat rigid and pale on her chair, the front of her nightgown growing damp from the milk leaking from her breasts. During that long, harrowing morning, Keith had been certain that Annie was close to complete despair, and that he was the strong one.

Afterward, Annie grieved. She mourned. She wept inconsolably. She spent hours upon hours in the vacant nursery, hovering over Adam's empty crib until Keith dismantled it and gave it to the Salvation Army. Within a week, he had also packed all of Adam's clothes and toys and given them to charity. Keith saw to the house, and Annie saw to her soul. Annie cried, and Keith remained dry-eyed.

One day, at the pediatrician's recommendation, Annie decided that she and Keith ought to attend a meeting of a support group for parents who had lost their children to SIDS. Hoping that it would improve Annie's spirits, Keith agreed to go with her. He and Annie sat in the living room of a large, air-conditioned ranch house in Chico, surrounded by other parents, and Annie and the others talked about their sorrow and frustration and helplessness. She seemed bolstered by the camaraderie, but Keith found the entire exercise ridiculous.

She continued to go to the support group meetings without Keith. And he began to think about leaving. Annie didn't need him anymore; she received the solace she required from her group. She was growing stronger, beginning to smile again, beginning to function. She didn't need Keith, and he was finding it harder and harder to stay.

So he left. He did it as fairly and rationally as he could. He reviewed the terms of the lease on their rented house with Annie, signed over their entire savings account to her, gave her the furniture, the pots and pans, everything except his clothing. He told her that he loved her but that he needed some time to himself. He was as honest as he had always been with her, totally honest.

His first stop was Berkeley, and the apartment he'd shared with two other guys during law school. They were both still working on their degrees, and they welcomed him back into the apartment, no questions asked. He had to sleep on the couch—another graduate student had taken over his former bedroom—but his friends didn't charge him any rent, and they didn't ask him what had happened between him and Annie, what had driven them apart.

Keith spent a few months there, drinking heavily, running through the few hundred dollars remaining in his checking account. Then he left, roaming farther south, landing a job harvesting tomatoes through one of his farmworker acquaintances. The mere idea of practicing law seemed untenable to Keith; all he wanted to do was toil and sweat and wash away his memories with a few ice-cold beers at the end of a long day.

The harvest ended in October and Keith moved on again. He could no longer remember all the towns he had visited, all the odd jobs he had taken. He spent a blustery winter in Denver, a torrid summer in New Orleans, months here and there, continually moving so that he wouldn't have to think too much.

One afternoon, while he was sitting on a park bench near the St. Louis Arch, staring at the slow-moving gray water of the Mississippi River, he heard a baby cry. If he had bothered to look, he would have found the source of the sound—a couple of tourists, one holding a squirming baby while the other took a photograph of the Arch. But Keith didn't look. He closed his eyes, listened, absorbed the sound, and heard himself whisper, "*My* son. He was *my* son, too."

And finally, miraculously, he was able to cry.

Annie arrived at the Brenton Motor Inn ten minutes late. She usually made a habit of being punctual, but tonight she was nervous. After she'd gotten home, she'd showered, washed her hair and tried on three different outfits before selecting a modest moss-green sweater dress with a high collar. Then she'd dried her hair, arranged it in a knot, grimaced and yanked out all the pins, opting instead to let it hang loose down her back. She'd applied the faintest touch of makeup to her face, fretted that it made her look strange, then did her best to convince herself that, in fact, it made her look polished and mature.

She had also spent an inordinate amount of time dialing her sister's telephone number and listening to the phone ring at the other end of the continent. Annie supposed that Teri had the right not to be home, but she couldn't help being irritated by her sister's failure to answer. Annie desperately wanted to hear Teri's version of Keith's trip to Portland, to hear if he'd really come close to torturing her, as he had claimed. Most of all, Annie wanted to find out why Teri had never informed her of his visit.

But Teri wasn't home by seven o'clock—four o'clock Portland time—and Annie couldn't stall any longer. Scared, intrigued and edgier than she thought possible, she drove to the motel at the western end of town.

Keith was waiting for her in the lobby. He had on a gray wool suit, superbly tailored to his tall body, a pale blue shirt and striped silk tie. His long hair was neatly parted and combed across his brow, and his black loafers were buffed. For a moment, Annie thought he looked like a model in an advertisement for an investment company, or for a yuppie cologne.

The notion caused her to grin. Keith LaMotte, a friend of the migrant laborers, a young, upwardly mobile professional? Her smile faded as she acknowledged the reality of the well-groomed man standing before her in the small, glass-walled motel lobby.

"What on earth have you been up to?" she asked with feigned disapproval. "You look like a banker or something."

"I'm a lawyer, remember?" he replied, holding the door open for her and then following her out into the balmy night.

"A lawyer, sure," Annie conceded, allowing him to usher her to his rental car and help her onto the seat. His gaze seemed to dawdle for a moment on her stockinged legs, and she realized that she, too, must look a bit more sophisticated than he remembered her to be. But the way she looked now was the maximum of sophistication for her. She couldn't shake the suspicion that Keith probably appeared this debonair a good deal of the time. "Something tells me," she continued once he had taken his seat behind the wheel, "that you aren't putting in too many unbilled hours with the United Farm Workers these days."

"Not as many as I used to," Keith confirmed. "Where are we going?"

Annie tried to gauge his tone. Was he deliberately evading her questions, or was he merely eager for directions to the restaurant? She navigated him onto a route that led to the interstate, then settled into the upholstery and appraised the man beside her. "Do you work for a law firm?" she asked, choosing to stick with her line of questioning.

He nodded. "I've been an associate with one of the big firms in L.A. for about two years."

"And before that?"

"I worked as an assistant in the D.A.'s office."

Annie's eyes sharpened on him. Was this the same Keith LaMotte who used to thumb his nose at bureaucrats and corporate grinds, who used to mock all his law school friends who were scrambling for internships and invitations to join the big-money firms? Was this the same Keith LaMotte who once worked twelve-hour days for weeks on end, preparing a class-action suit against a grower who refused to provide his pickers with access to fresh drinking water?

"What did you do before you worked in the D.A.'s office?" she asked cautiously. She couldn't believe Keith had left Orland and moved directly into such a high-pressure environment. He must have done something else first, to ease the transition.

He didn't answer immediately. He pretended to be engrossed in the road signs directing him onto the highway. Once he had followed the winding entrance ramp and merged into the southbound lane, he shot Annie a quick look. "Before I worked in the D.A.'s office, I was a bum," he said blandly.

Certain she'd heard him incorrectly, she reiterated, "A bum?"

"That's right."

She waited for him to elaborate. When he didn't, she asked, "What kind of bum?"

He chuckled wryly. "How many kinds are there, Annie? I grew a beard, had no permanent address and drank too much. Is this the exit I ought to take?"

Stunned by his blunt confession, she had forgotten to pay attention to the road. "Yes," she said hastily, causing him to swerve into the exit lane at high speed. The sharp turn tossed her in his direction; if she hadn't been wearing a seat belt, she might have fallen into his arms.

Into the arms of a bum, she pondered. A salvaged bum, a redeemed ex-bum. For reasons she thought best not to examine, she found the idea oddly arousing.

"Why—" she began, then cleared the roughness from her throat. "Why did you tell Tim Shandler you were my husband?"

Keith shot her another brief look, then mumbled something unintelligible beneath his breath. "Where's the restaurant?"

"Answer me first," Annie demanded.

Keith braked to a stop on the shoulder of the road, then twisted in his seat to face her. "Because you wore my ring," he said, each word hard and uninflected. "Now, tell me where the damned restaurant is, Annie, or else..."

He left the threat dangling. Annie gazed into his eyes, which were even darker in the evening's shadows, and wished she had the nerve to ask him what he would do if she didn't tell him where the restaurant was. But she was afraid—afraid she'd loathe what he said, afraid she'd like it. "Follow this road to the first light and make a left," she said in a muted voice. "It's a French restaurant. I made a reservation."

He continued to stare at her for a moment, his eyes piercing the darkness, his chest rising and falling in a constant rhythm as he breathed. She expected him to turn away, to shift into gear and drive to the restaurant. Instead, he extended his arm and cupped his hand around her cheek.

"It was almost like being married, wasn't it?" he whispered.

Annie opened and then closed her mouth. She didn't know what to say—and even if she did, she doubted she'd be able to shape the words. Keith's hand was so gentle as he molded it to her face, as he held her head steady. For a fleeting instant she did remember everything: the approximation of marriage, the sensation of Keith's mouth on hers, the delirious love she'd felt for him, both physical and emotional. She remembered everything she had promised herself to forget, and if Keith didn't let go of her soon, it would be too late. The memories she'd fought so hard to vanquish would be back again, forever.

But he did let go of her, returned his hand to the steering wheel and released the parking brake. "Left at the light," he repeated as he eased back into the flow of traffic.

Why? Why was he here? Why had he found her? Well into their dinner, the question that Keith hadn't answered—the question that evidently he couldn't answer—continued to haunt Annie.

They were seated at a relatively secluded table, where the chief source of lighting was a candle with a jittery golden flame. The waiters were discreet, the menu printed in a barely readable script, the dishes described in recipe detail, with the ingredients and seasonings listed and the manner of cooking identified. Annie ought to have appreciated the ambience, the service, the food. But she was too distracted by Keith, by the fact that he was sitting all of three feet away from her, across a narrow linen-covered table; by the fact that he had said, "It was almost like being married, wasn't it?"; by the fact that his hand had felt so good against her cheek.

She almost wished they didn't have a history. As she asked him to describe his current work—mostly litigation, he told her, defending people accused of white-collar crimes and pressing damage claims—she wished she could listen impartially, as if she were meeting Keith for the first time. She wished that this was, in fact, a date and nothing more, a chance for her to get acquainted with the handsome, dark-eyed new man in town. More than once she was hard-pressed to remember that she had once lived with him, that they'd shared a bed, that they'd created a child.

"Enough about me," he announced after describing a case he'd recently won involving a landlord-tenant dispute. That Keith had represented the tenant reassured Annie, even though the tenant was a multimillionaire renting an ocean-front villa in Malibu. "Let's talk about you."

Annie didn't want to talk about herself. She dropped her gaze to the nearly empty plate in front of her and tried to recall what delicious entrée had been on it. She'd managed to consume it, but she'd been so engrossed in Keith's description of his work that she'd forgotten to pay attention to what she'd been eating.

"Why library science?" he asked.

She smiled tentatively. She considered telling Keith that she wasn't obligated to explain herself, that she wasn't the one who had imposed on him and, therefore, that she didn't have to answer his questions.

But she and Keith *did* have a history—a passionate, painful one, a history once defined by love and respect. Because of their history, she owed him something. "I like books," she said.

"Obviously. You were an English major." He broke off a piece of crust from his dinner roll, dabbed it with butter and popped it into his mouth. "It must have been more than liking books, though," he commented.

She shrugged and leaned back in her chair. "Library work seemed like something I'd enjoy. I've always felt comfortable in libraries, Keith. I like being surrounded by all those great literary works—and all the blockbusters, too. I like the way books feel, and smell. And it's such an orderly world. Everything is systematic. I like that.''

Keith studied her. He seemed to probe her with his eyes, fascinated but somewhat skeptical. ''It's been a long time since I've ventured into a children's library, Annie, but my memory of them is that they weren't all that orderly. Kids aren't very good at keeping their voices down.''

Annie shrugged again, this time smiling indulgently. ''In the children's library here in Brenton, we don't bother trying to keep them quiet,'' she confessed. ''We have a pet parakeet and a little play corner filled with toys.''

''Why?'' Keith asked, suddenly solemn. ''Why a *children's* librarian?''

Annie pressed her lips together as she mulled over her answer. She could tell him the truth—that she'd chosen that specialty because she hoped it would make her accept children as a natural part of her world. For years after Adam's death, she hadn't been able to look at children without resenting them, envying their mothers, cursing herself and her pitiful luck. Only by surrounding herself with children, and by forcing herself to contend with them on a regular basis, did she think she'd be able to overcome her loss.

She could tell Keith that—but she wouldn't. ''I like children,'' she said simply.

As if such a statement could be simple passing from her to Keith. A shadow crossed his eyes and a muscle near the hinge of his jaw twitched. Then he willed himself to relax. ''Do you want dessert?'' he asked, abruptly changing the subject.

''I wouldn't mind hearing what they've got,'' she replied. She understood his reaction; she was happy to abandon the topic of children for something as irrelevant as dessert.

Keith summoned the waiter, who dutifully recited a sinful list of sweets. Despite the waiter's mouth-watering descriptions, Annie realized she wasn't hungry. Saying that she liked children and comprehending the discomfort her words had caused Keith had stolen what was left of her appetite. Thanking the waiter, she declined dessert.

Keith asked for the check. A heavy silence blanketed them as they waited for the waiter to bring it, as Keith reviewed it and handed the waiter his credit card, as he signed the receipt, stood and circled the table to help Annie out of her chair. He made no move to take her arm as they wove among the tables to the door, and then outside.

The night was mild, the harvest moon fat and peach-colored, hanging low in the sky. Annie and Keith strolled side by side across the gravel parking lot, she clutching her purse and he plunging his hands into the pockets of his trousers. At the car, he poked the key into the passenger door lock, then abandoned it and straightened up.

Even in her high heels Annie stood a few inches shorter than Keith. Her eyes were level with his chin, and she recalled, as she had at Shandler's that afternoon, the way his jaw used to feel against her fingers, the thick ridge of it, the hard shape, the faint scratchiness of his skin in the morning when they used to lie in bed, the early sunlight spilling onto them through the ineffectual curtains adorning the windows. She would run her fingers over the bristly surface, and even if Keith hadn't been awake, her caress would rouse him. And they'd kiss....

"You're prettier than I remembered," he said.

Annie's face grew warm. She wondered if Keith had read her mind, if he was aware of the sensual turn her thoughts had taken.

She laughed nervously to cover her embarrassment. "You remember me fat, don't you?"

"I remember..." He touched her cheek again, tracing the bone beneath her eye and then the soft hollow below. "I remember that you were beautiful, but not so pretty. I wasn't just being polite when I said you look terrific, Annie. You do."

"Thank you."

"It's complicating things," he warned her.

"What things?" Her voice sounded airy, unable to support itself. She wished he'd keep his hand to himself so that she would be able to think straight.

"I didn't come all this way to make a pass at you," Keith murmured, sliding his fingers back past her temple and deep into her hair. "But right now, that's exactly what I want to do."

Before she could stop him, he bowed and brushed his mouth over hers.

Three

___

He moved his lips slowly against hers, pressing and then, just when she grew used to the pressure, relenting. There was something careful in his motions, something contained. The passionate clenching of his fingers in her hair as he held her head steady beneath his was the only evidence that his control was the least bit shaky.

He pulled back, and Annie opened her mouth to speak, even though she had no idea what she wanted to say. At the parting of her lips, he bowed to her again, sliding his tongue gently along the surface of her teeth. He lifted his free hand to her shoulder and then to the side of her neck, stroking the skin behind her earlobe. She sighed, and he deepened the kiss.

Sighing again as their tongues met, she reached for his shoulders. She reveled in the solidity of him, the hard shelves of bone and muscle beneath the expensive wool of his jacket. She celebrated his height, his strength, the inviting smell of him—not the scent of some cologne, but a richer, distinctly male scent. As she molded her fingers to him, he groaned softly and tightened his hold on her.

She wasn't sure what, if anything, she had expected to find in his kiss: a sense of welcome, of familiarity, a blazing reunion, an intrusion of memory. What she felt was totally different. It was new, strange, alarmingly erotic. The touch of Keith's lips had an amazing effect on her. His mouth mastered hers with sweeping strokes and demoralizing withdrawals. The tantalizing thrusts of his tongue ignited a yearning deep inside her, her body resonating in sympathy with her mouth. Just when she ached for him he slipped away, then tilted his head a fraction of an inch and plunged even deeper, his tongue a sensual marauder seeking worlds to conquer.

This was nothing like the kisses she and Keith used to share. Those had been juicy, affectionate, sometimes utterly abandoned. What Keith was doing to her now he was doing willfully, cleverly. He wasn't a man carried away by his love for a woman; he was a man performing a seduction.

Frightened by the realization—and even more frightened by the extent to which she was responding—Annie jerked her head away. She inhaled a ragged gasp of air and closed her eyes so that she wouldn't have to see him. "Don't," she whispered brokenly.

He relaxed his hands, weaving his fingers through her hair and brushing it back from her feverish cheeks. He dropped one arm and looped it around her waist, urged her tentatively against himself in a comforting hug, then released her when she stiffened in self-defense. Taking a respectful step backward, he mumbled, "I'm sorry."

"Stop saying you're sorry," she snapped, opening her eyes, feeling safer now that he wasn't standing so close to her. "You were sorry when you snuck up on me at Shandler's. Now you're sorry for kissing me. If you're so damned sorry, Keith, why the hell are you here?''

"Annie—''

"You don't even know, do you?'' she snapped, refusing him a chance to explain. All her fury and confusion boiled over, emerging in a torrent of angry words. "You trail me like some sort of bloodhound, you harass my sister, you come barging into my life and interrupt me when I'm telling stories, and you sweep me off to dinner and say, 'Uh-oh, now I'm going to make a pass at you!' You expect it to be like old times, Keith. But it can't be, and it isn't.''

"Of course not,'' he said, his tone as hushed as hers was enraged. "Everything's changed. Kissing you has changed, too. I didn't expect it to be the same, Annie. Did you?''

She stared at him, stunned. Her heavy breathing gradually returned to normal as she read the honesty in his dark, deep-set eyes. She forced herself to meet his gaze, and she forced herself to match his honesty. "Maybe,'' she confessed in a small, tortured voice, "maybe I did expect it to be the same.''

As soon as she spoke the words she understood their truth. Her anger had arisen less from the fact that Keith had kissed her than from the *way* he'd kissed her. It hadn't been like the kisses she remembered. It had been more skilled, more practiced, more deliberate. He hadn't had a discernible technique when they were lovers so many years ago, but he did now. Annie knew intuitively that he'd learned his technique—from someone else, from other women.

For a brief, insane moment she was jealous.

Keith stood silently, watching the flicker of emotions dance across her face. Unable to decipher them, he exhaled. "Spit it out, Annie. If you're mad at me for kissing you, fair enough. Just spit it out.''

"Who did you learn to kiss like that from?'' she asked, averting her gaze. She could be as honest with Keith as he was with her, but she lacked the nerve to look him in the eye when she was being so honest.

She could sense more than see his lips spreading in a smile. "Oh, Annie," he murmured, amusement tinging his words. "It's been an awfully long time. Was I supposed to be saving myself for tonight?"

"Don't ask me," she retorted. She folded her arms protectively across her chest and paced a few steps, putting some more distance between her and Keith. "I didn't know there was going to be a 'tonight' for you to save yourself for."

"All right," he said, honoring her need for space by remaining where he was while she walked out her agitation. He leaned against the bumper of the car, watching her, measuring her temper. "True confessions, Annie. I haven't been a monk in the past six years."

Of course he hadn't; she hadn't expected him to be one. She hadn't expected ever to see him again. What did she care that he'd been with other women since they'd parted ways?

Her anger began to ebb, replaced by an aching wistfulness. True confessions. When she and Keith had been together, right up to the end, they had always been this frank with each other.

They had never hidden anything. "True confessions," Keith would say before admitting that he thought the rhubarb pie Annie had slaved over for hours tasted like rags soaked in sewer water. "True confessions," Annie would declare before telling Keith that his refusal to sort the garbage into recyclable and nonrecyclable piles irritated her no end.

She had never known such honesty with anyone else, not even her sister. Certainly not with another man. She missed it. After all these years she still missed it.

"True confessions, Keith," she said aloud, pivoting to face him. "Why are you here?"

"I wish I knew," he said, the humor-filled sparkle fading from his eyes. "Believe me, if I did I'd tell you."

"Are you planning to stay until you figure it out?" she asked apprehensively.

"Yes."

"How long do you think it's going to take?"

"I don't know, Annie," he said, extending his arm to her. "And I don't care."

She eyed his hand dubiously, refusing to take it. "What about your job? What about your fancy law firm in L.A.?"

"I've been jobless before, plenty of times," he said. "This is more important."

"What is more important? Badgering me? Playing games with me?"

He let his arm drop and glanced down at the loose gravel surrounding his feet. "A few minutes ago I believed that kissing you was the most important thing in the world. I didn't know you were going to be turned off by it."

"I wasn't," Annie conceded in a whisper. "I wasn't at all. It just . . . it was different from the way we used to kiss."

"Everything's different, Annie. And maybe that's for the best." Pushing himself away from the car, he twisted the key in the lock and opened the door for her.

They drove home in silence. Annie ruminated about what had happened outside the restaurant, what Keith had done, what he'd said. She had no right to be jealous of the fact that he hadn't been a monk—except that she herself had been celibate, a few heated kisses notwithstanding. She was jealous not of the women Keith had known but of Keith himself, for having known other lovers while Annie had been alone.

Legally or not, she and Keith had been married. Now Annie was the ex-wife, struggling along in solitude while Keith enjoyed a healthy sex life. Maybe the only reason she'd responded to him as strongly as she had was that it had been such a long time since she'd been kissed by a man.

No. She had responded to Keith because he was Keith. She didn't love him—she hadn't loved him for six years—but at one time they had shared a beautiful, mutually satisfying sexual relationship. She yearned to experience something like it again, but so far it simply hadn't happened.

For the first time since Keith had left, she forced herself to acknowledge all the things she had lost along with him. Like the taste of his lips and the feel of his fingers floating through her hair as he held her. Like the throbbing in her heart, in her womb, the desire for him to fill her with himself. Like the sense of completion she'd found with him and nobody else.

She didn't love Keith, and she didn't miss him. But she missed being in love with him.

"Hey, Annie!" a familiar high-pitched voice called out, destroying the silence.

Annie glanced up from the computer terminal sitting on top of the counter in the children's library, which occupied the basement level of the Brenton Town Library. Across the counter from Annie stood Justine Willis, a smudge-nosed seven-year-old with a tangled mane of brown hair and a voice shrill enough to shatter crystal five miles away. Justine was wearing a zippered sweat jacket over her plaid blouse and corduroy slacks. She gripped a Charlie Brown schoolbag in one of her hands and a cellophane package of potato chips in the other.

"Hello, Justine," Annie said without much enthusiasm, and switched off the computer. As long as Justine was in the library, Annie wouldn't be able to get her work done. "Where's your mother?"

"She told me to come here straight from school today," Justine squawked, flinging her schoolbag onto the counter with a proprietary nonchalance that never failed to irritate Annie. Then she hoisted herself up to sit on the counter, and started swinging her legs and kicking the front of it. "She said she's got to have her hair done this afternoon, so I should just come straight here and do my homework."

"Then maybe you ought to do your homework," Annie said, trying not to sound exasperated. "And please don't sit on the counter, Justine. It isn't a chair." To drive the point home, she gave Justine's rear end an emphatic nudge. Justine obediently leaped down, landing neatly on her sneakered feet.

It wasn't really Justine's fault that her mother had designated Annie to be her unpaid baby-sitter. Madelyn Willis deposited Justine at the children's library at least twice a week—usually more often. Annie didn't know much about Madelyn Willis, but she knew more than she wanted to know about Justine. Ever since mid-July, Justine had been a fixture in the library. Annie had hoped that her visits would become less frequent once school started, but they didn't. As soon as the huge electric clock above the door read two-thirty, Annie braced herself for Justine's afterschool appearance. Only if she made it to four o'clock without having to see Justine did Annie consider herself safe for the day.

"And while we're on the subject of things you're not supposed to do in the library," Annie reproached, fearing that she sounded like a first-class nag, "you know you're not allowed to eat potato chips in here."

Justine unzipped her jacket and pulled it off. "I brought these for the parakeet," she said, scampering toward the bird cage, which stood on a pedestal near one of the small high windows.

"Birds don't eat potato chips," Annie called after her, but she was too late. Justine had torn open the bag and was poking chips between the bars of the cage. The traitorous bird gobbled them up with gusto.

"You'll never guess what happened in school today," Justine jabbered as she continued feeding the parakeet.

"Fine, I'll never guess," Annie muttered under her breath. Out loud, she said, "Justine, I'm really sorry, I've got work to do here. When you're done playing with the bird, why don't you go into the reading room and do your homework?"

"I'd rather talk."

"Not an option," Annie countered. "I'm working." With that, she sat back down on her upholstered swivel chair, clicked on the computer, and called up the file of overdue books.

Sending out overdue notices wasn't such an imperative task—and now that the library was computerized, it wasn't an arduous one, either. But Annie wasn't in the mood to shoot the breeze with Justine. She felt sorry for the little girl—Annie understood that Justine was lonely, and that her mother all but ignored her. But today, of all days, Annie simply couldn't entertain a demanding child.

She had finally reached Teri by telephone the previous night. "Sorry you had trouble getting hold of me," Teri said when Annie told her she'd tried her Saturday evening and all day Sunday. "Craig and I went on this incredible weekend in the mountains. Have I told you about Craig? He's an oral surgeon. My next-door neighbor's car broke down a couple of weeks ago, and I offered to take her kid to have an impacted molar pulled, and that's when I met Craig. I tell you, Annie, one look into his eyes and I wasn't sure who was getting the anesthesia, Marcie or me."

"And you went away with him? For a weekend?" Annie was happy to let her sister share her news first.

"Well, you don't have to make it sound so sleazy," Teri said haughtily. "Craig and I have been seeing each other for some time now. We've spent nearly every evening together since he did Marcie's extraction. It isn't like we're strangers."

"I didn't say it was sleazy," Annie protested. The fact was, Teri had always had a much more colorful love life than Annie. Annie was the old-married type; why else would she have settled down with Keith at the absurdly young age of twenty-two? She envied Teri, and she enjoyed Teri's romances vicariously. "I'm sure it was all quite respectable," she said placatingly.

"Not *too* respectable," Teri countered with a sly giggle. She proceeded to enumerate Craig's many assets, from his wonderfully curly hair to his brilliance at translating Sartre's philosophy into language even Teri could understand, from his adorable ski cabin—where they didn't go skiing because there wasn't enough snow—to his reputation around Portland for relatively painless tooth extractions. "So how come you've been calling me all weekend?" Teri asked when she finally ran out of praises to heap on her new beloved.

"Keith is here," Annie said.

"Oh." Teri lapsed into a temporary silence. "Keith is there?"

"He's in Brenton."

Another silence, and then Teri said, "Hey, Annie, it's not my fault. I swear—I didn't tell him where you were."

"I know you didn't. He found me on his own," Annie reported. "But Teri, why didn't you tell me he went to Oregon to see you?"

"It was a long time ago," Teri defended herself. "A couple of years ago, at least. You weren't in such good shape then, Annie, and—"

"Damn it, Teri, you should have told me."

Teri let out a long breath. "Annie . . . well, you loved him so much, and he hurt you so badly. I was afraid if I told you he was looking for you, you might be flattered, and then you'd start feeling sentimental about him, and then you'd forget all about what a bastard he was."

Teri was right. Long after Annie had assured her sister that everything was fine, that she had matters well under control with Keith, long after she'd hung up and climbed into bed, she tried to remember what a bastard he had been. All she'd come up with was his honesty, his unflagging honesty. And the hunger his kiss had unleashed within her. And his disarming vulnerability, his doubt and bemusement every time he said, "I don't know, Annie."

He was in trouble. She didn't know why, but she sensed that he was lost, rudderless, searching not for Annie herself but for something else, something he hoped to find with her, or in her.

The dinner, the conversation, the kiss—all of that might fall under the heading of courtship. But he hadn't come to Brenton to court her. She knew it, and so did he.

"Hey, Annie, the bird really loves these chips!" Justine shrieked. "He's gobbling them up like crazy."

Annie grimaced, wondering about the effect salty, greasy potato chips would have on the poor parakeet's stomach. She forced a smile for the young woman leading a toddler down the steps into the library, carrying a stack of picture books. The woman dropped them off on the return table and wandered with her child into the book room. The toddler raced to the play corner while the mother busied herself scouring the picture book shelves.

Justine watched the mother and child for a minute, then returned to the counter. She unbuckled her schoolbag. "I got an A on my arithmetic test," she boasted to Annie. "Wanna see?"

Not really, Annie answered silently. Out loud, she said, "Justine, I've got to get my work done. Why don't you save the test to show your mother?"

"She doesn't care," Justine said blithely, thrusting a sheet of ditto paper at Annie, who dutifully glanced at it. "How about that? Maybe I'll be a mathematician when I grow up. What do mathematicians do, Annie?"

"They sit very quietly and don't bother the librarian," Annie answered promptly. "They do their homework and let the librarian fill out the overdue notices."

"You gonna add up the fines?" Justine asked, leaning far over the counter in an attempt to read the computer monitor. "I could add 'em up for you. I'm real good at adding."

Annie checked the urge to scream. No way was she going to lose her temper in front of Keith, whom she'd just spotted as he swung open the outer door and started down the stairs. He had to duck to avoid hitting his head on the low ceiling above the upper part of the staircase. His hair was windblown, and he'd shoved up the sleeves of the pullover sweater he was wearing. He smiled as he approached the counter.

"Hello," he whispered.

Annie gazed at Keith. She hadn't seen him on Sunday, but she'd known that he was still in Brenton, and she'd suspected that he would remain in Brenton for at least a few more days. Still, his appearance in the children's library Monday afternoon was almost as distracting as his appearance at Shandler's on Saturday. She simply wasn't used to his being around.

More than that, she wasn't used to seeing him smile so brightly. The smile shaping his lips today wasn't like the shy, tenuous smiles he'd given her Saturday. This one was full and radiant, carving dimples into his cheeks.

Dimples. Of all Keith's attributes, Annie often believed that his dimples alone had been responsible for winning her heart. She loved the way they creased his cheeks, the way they framed his mouth and made him look boyish and charming and sweet.

Tearing her eyes from his face, she found Justine's attention riveted to the meeting unfolding before her. Her saucer-eyed stare passed from Annie to Keith and back to Annie. "Is this your boyfriend?" she screeched, loud enough for the mother and toddler in the play area to hear. Loud enough, Annie feared, for the mayor of Hartford to hear.

Doing her best to maintain her composure, Annie tucked a loose strand of hair behind her ear and said, in a muted voice, "He's a friend of mine, Justine, and if you don't turn the volume down, I'm going to put a muzzle on you."

Keith's eyes widened. Annie wondered whether he was reacting to her tone—but his comment informed her that he was more impressed by something else she'd said: "Do I really qualify as a friend?"

"For the time being," Annie said brusquely. "Now, if you don't mind, I've got work to do." She turned her back on Keith and Justine, happy to ignore them both, and dropped onto her swivel chair in front of the computer monitor.

"You wanna see the bird?" Justine asked Keith. *Any port in the storm,* Annie thought wryly.

Keith's smile was apparently a reflection of his mood. "Sure," he said amiably. "Let's see the bird. What's your name?"

"Justine Willis. What's yours?"

"Keith LaMotte." He let her take his hand and drag him to the cage below the window. "What's the bird's name?"

"He doesn't have one. You know what? He likes potato chips. I just fed him a whole bag of potato chips. I think Annie's sore about it," Justine added in a stage whisper.

"Potato chips, huh." Keith inspected the trilling bird. "Why not call him Mr. Chips?"

"Okay!" Justine hooted. "Hey, Annie—"

"Keep it down, will you?" Annie scolded in an irritable whisper. She punched a few keys on the computer to give the impression of being hard at work.

"Hey, Annie," Justine hollered, a half a decibel lower, "is it all right if we call the bird Mr. Chips?"

"Be my guests," Annie said shortly.

Keith studied Annie for a minute, then turned to Justine. "I think she doesn't want to be bothered right now," he observed sagely. "Maybe you ought to leave her alone."

"But I haven't got anybody else to talk to!" Justine whined.

"You can talk to me," Keith offered. "Quietly, though. Why don't we sit over there?" He pointed to one of the tables near the play corner.

"That's where the babies go," Justine sulked, curling her lip.

As if on cue, the young mother and toddler left the play area for the counter, where Annie checked out a few more picture books for them. They left, and the play area was unoccupied.

"Come on," Keith said, urging Justine toward the table. "Let's try to stay out of Annie's hair." Reluctantly, Justine picked up her schoolbag and joined Keith at the table.

Annie continued working on the overdue slips, filling out the preprinted postcards with book and record titles and calculations of fines. Every now and then, she risked a surreptitious glimpse in Keith's direction. The chair he sat on was designed for children, and his tall body looked absurd folded up on the tiny seat, with his knees bent into acute angles and his head and shoulders towering above the seat back. Justine sat next to him, solemnly explaining the contents of one of her textbooks, which she'd removed from her schoolbag. Keith was doing a decent job of appearing fascinated by Justine's lecture.

Annie grinned in astonishment. No doubt Keith's tolerance for Justine was based on his not having had to contend with her several times a week for upward of four months. But even at that, Annie had trouble believing that he could so effectively keep an obnoxious little girl entertained. Even as a father, he hadn't been the sort to melt at the sight of a cute child. He hadn't played much with Adam, claiming that Adam wasn't old enough to play with, and he'd changed Adam's diapers only when Annie wasn't available. He liked Adam, or at least he loved him. But he wasn't a "child" person.

Annie mulled over the possibility that Keith was keeping Justine occupied only as a favor to Annie. Yet, he didn't owe Annie any favors—or if he did, they were so enormous that steering Justine out of Annie's path for a couple of hours would hardly count for much. Besides, he didn't seem to be faking his interest in Justine. He seemed authentically captivated by her.

Annie decided not to question Keith's motives. She decided not to think at all about his presence in the library. Instead, she bowed over her work, filling out the overdue notices, taking advantage of the peace that had settled over her domain.

By a quarter to five, she was finished with the postcards. She wrapped them in a rubber band and shut off the computer. Swiveling in her chair, she found Justine hunched over an arithmetic workbook and Keith attempting to lean back in his chair as he perused a large hardcover book. His legs were stretched out in front of him, one ankle resting on the other knee, and his expression was rapt. Annie wondered what he was reading.

The click of high heels on the steps drew Annie's attention from Keith. She turned to see Justine's mother descending the stairs, her reddish hair permed into chic round curls. "Hi, Annie," Madelyn Willis greeted her with a carefree smile. "Is Justine here?"

"Yes, she is." Annie nodded toward the table near the play corner.

"Justine, darling. Mommy's here," Madelyn announced, opening her arms to the girl.

Justine eyed her mother, curved her lips in a modest smile, and folded her workbook shut. Rather than rushing into her mother's outstretched arms, she took her time packing up her schoolbag and pulling on her jacket. Not until her mother finally let her hands fall to her sides did Justine rise from her chair and stroll around the table to Madelyn.

Keith had stood at Madelyn's entrance. The curly-haired woman gave him a curious inspection, then smiled and took Justine's hand. "Were you a good girl today?" she asked.

"Uh-huh," Justine reported. "I got an A on my arithmetic test."

"Good for you!" Madelyn planted a loud kiss on Justine's cheek, then started with her toward the stairs. "Thanks for keeping an eye on her, Annie," she called breezily over her shoulder before leading her daughter out of the library.

Pressing her lips together, Annie watched their departure. When the door swung shut, she turned to find Keith nearing the counter. "Thanks," Annie said wearily, pulling her keys from a pocket of her skirt and locking the file drawers under the counter.

"For what?"

"For putting up with her. She gets on my nerves, sometimes."

"So I gathered." He watched as Annie methodically closed down her work space, covering the computer with a dustcover, setting the postcards into the basket for outgoing mail, then emerging from behind the counter to fill the parakeet's food dish for the night. "Any particular reason she bothers you?" he asked.

"She's too loud."

"You told me you don't really care about noise in the library," he reminded her.

Annie yielded with a nod. "I guess what bothers me is that her mother uses me as a baby-sitting service. I think that girl spends more time here than she does at her own house. Just because her mother's a taxpayer doesn't mean she can exploit the town's employees that way."

"It's her mother you ought to be ticked off at, not the kid," Keith noted sensibly.

Annie slid the refilled food dish into the bird cage and rotated back to Keith. "You're right," she conceded. "But the kid's the one I've got to deal with all the time."

"She's dying for attention," Keith surmised.

Annie's eyes narrowed on him. Since when had he become a child psychology expert? Since when had he become sensitive to the needs of school-age kids?

Keith had clearly undergone some major changes in the past few years. Having spent time as a bum was the least of it.

Once again, she was brimming with questions, questions she wasn't sure how to ask. She settled for an easy one: "What were you reading so intently while Justine did her homework?"

"*McElligot's Pool*. Dr. Seuss."

"A classic," Annie said, praising his choice.

"I like the philosophy it espouses," Keith remarked. "It advises you to wait, to be patient and cool."

"And to dream," Annie concluded, momentarily caught up in his analysis of the book. But she didn't want to discuss philosophy with Keith. They'd spent plenty of their idealistic youth philosophizing about the Meaning of Life— and a lot of good it did them, she thought with a sniff.

"Well," she said crisply, returning to the counter for her purse. "It's closing time."

"Do you have any plans for tonight?"

She paused to sort her thoughts. She wasn't sure it was a good idea to have dinner with Keith again. If she did, and then she had dinner with him tomorrow, and the next day, she'd grow accustomed to his company. And then, when he left for Los Angeles, she'd feel doubly lonely.

If she had dinner with him tonight, he might kiss her again.

She could use a little romance in her life. No question about that. But not with Keith.

She began to tell him she was booked for the evening, but as soon as she raised her eyes to his the words stuck in her throat. She couldn't lie to Keith. She never had been able to before; she couldn't now.

"The only plan I have," she told him, "is to eat dinner and go to bed. But I intend to do it alone."

"Do what alone?" he asked, grinning playfully. "Eat or go to bed?"

"Both," she said curtly.

"Let's compromise," he suggested. "Eat dinner with me, and I'll let you go to bed alone."

She scrutinized him warily, unsure of how seriously he wanted his comment to be taken. Did he actually think she would consider going to bed with him? They'd exchanged one simple kiss two nights ago, that was all.

One kiss—but it had hardly been simple. That one kiss had reminded Annie of how hollow her life was. It had spoken of the years that had passed since she'd last been in love.

Keith wasn't the only person who had changed since then, Annie acknowledged. She'd changed, too. She was no longer the same person she'd been the last time she had kissed Keith. Her half of the kiss had been as different as his.

She didn't want to go to bed with him—but she wanted, irrationally, to regress seven or eight years, to go back to the beginning, when she was young and, she believed, indestructible, when she foolishly thought she could depend on Keith for better or worse, forever.

She wanted to be the person she used to be, and make love to the person Keith used to be. But she knew that, no matter how long one waited, no matter how patient and cool one was, certain dreams wouldn't come true.

"I think we'd better skip dinner, too," she remembered to answer Keith. "I think it would be best."

Disappointment cut across his strong features—and then vanished to be replaced by determination. "All right," he granted. "You can eat dinner alone."

He unrolled the sleeves of his shirt, buttoned the cuffs and pulled down his sweater sleeves over them. Then he helped Annie on with her wool-lined windbreaker. They climbed the stairs together, Keith remembering to duck his head when he reached the top two steps. He waited while she locked the outer door, accompanied her to the parking lot behind the library, and saw her into her car. Once she was seated behind the wheel, he closed the door for her, waved, and sauntered away.

He seemed awfully unruffled by the possibility that he would never see Annie again. Rather than being hurt by his attitude, she was suspicious. No sooner had she left the parking lot when her suspicions bore fruit. In her rearview mirror she spotted his rented Pontiac cruising close behind her back bumper.

She braked at a stop sign and puzzled through her reeling emotions. Should she pull over, climb out and ask him to leave her alone? Should she warn him that if he continued to tail her she'd report him to the police?

Or should she let him follow her home? Should she let him invade the sanctity of her house? Should she hear him out?

Sighing, she shifted into gear and drove through the intersection. Keith followed.

Her house was a couple of miles from the center of town. It was a modest two-bedroom shingled ranch house on a small, grassy lot, and she was currently renting it with an option to buy, if her income ever increased enough for her to qualify for a mortgage. Her landlord had recently retired on a comfortable pension, and he was in no rush to sell the house.

She pulled into the driveway, and Keith parked by the overgrown curb. She turned off the engine, climbed out of her car, and stormed across the lawn to him. She had decided to let him follow her, but she wasn't exactly thrilled with her decision.

"What now?" she asked, planting her hands on her hips and glowering at him.

He grinned. "All you said was you wanted to eat by yourself and go to bed by yourself. You didn't say we couldn't talk."

"About what?"

"About my new job, here in Brenton."

Four

——

He had wondered, all day Sunday, whether when Annie had first arrived in Brenton the town had had as bewitching an effect on her as it had on him. He'd wondered whether he would have been as charmed by Brenton if he hadn't visited in October, when the foliage of southern New England was at its peak in color, the air was dry and mild and the breezes carried the scent of tart apples and pine. Perhaps, if he'd been able to track Annie down sooner and he'd arrived in Brenton during the March rains or the oppressive July mugginess, he might not have felt so strongly that he belonged here.

Then again, he might have, regardless of the season.

Rural Connecticut villages were nothing at all like the farming hamlets of California. Keith's vagabond years hadn't included any time in New England, but he knew enough about the region to have expected that the town would center around a quaint town green. Brenton's green was rectangular, crisscrossed with paved walks and dotted with towering trees. Genteel shops—among them a bookstore, a gourmet deli, several clothing boutiques and an old-fashioned hardware store with sawdust strewn across its floor—lined the sides of the green, and two competing churches—one Catholic, the other Presbyterian—stood at opposite ends. A solid brick building which housed the post office stood next to the Catholic church, a white clapboard building labeled "Town Hall" stood next to the Presbyterian church, and the pillared library had the southeastern corner of the green all to itself.

Brenton was different from California—cooler, more verdant, more self-contained. There was a certain intangible formality about the town—something modest and understated in the way people dressed, something reserved in their smiles. Keith was left with the impression that people respected each other's privacy here, that the shutters on the windows of all the houses symbolized something beyond an architectural aesthetic.

It struck him as odd that a born-and-bred Californian would feel so much at home in such an unfamiliar environment. But he did. The town seemed to welcome him—and it was clean. Not only was the air free of smog, but the streets were devoid of litter. The houses were freshly painted, the lawns mowed. Tree limbs had the good sense to curve neatly around the telephone wires that were strung above the sidewalks.

Brenton was the sort of town he and Annie used to dream of living in, back in their school days. Not that they'd imagined themselves moving across the country to New England, but Brenton boasted the attributes they wanted: tranquility, community, accessibility and unpolluted air.

All these years later, Annie had fulfilled their dream. Keith, on the other hand, was living in an overpriced apartment in Pasadena and working in an office tower with a dismal view of the traffic on Wilshire Boulevard. He didn't belong there. He belonged in Brenton, like Annie. The realization stunned him—and then elated him. He anticipated that Annie wouldn't be quite as elated as he was—at least not right away. But he hoped she'd be pleased.

"What job?" she asked warily.

He didn't answer. He was too curious about her house. He had figured out that she didn't want him to see it—why else would she have offered to pick him up at the motel Saturday night?—but he couldn't guess why. It was a lovely house: small and tidy with weathered gray shingles, a redbrick chimney, and black shutters and trim. The lawn was beginning to fade to a wintery pallor and the driveway was riven with cracks through which crabgrass was sprouting, but Keith liked the house.

"What job?" she repeated, digging her hands into the pockets of her skirt.

Keith turned from the house to study Annie. A gust of wind lifted her hair away from her face, revealing the exquisite sculptured line of her cheek and the sprinkle of freckles across it. It wasn't just the pristine beauty of Brenton that made Keith want to stay, but if he told Annie the more important reason, he'd probably frighten her. Better not to mention how strongly attracted he was to her, and how incredibly good he had felt when he'd kissed her Saturday night. The kiss obviously hadn't felt nearly as good to her as to him. He'd be wise to stick to the subject of his potential job opportunity for now.

"Invite me in," he said, "and I'll tell you all about it."

Annie measured him with her gaze. Then she sighed in resignation and started across the lawn to the front door. She hadn't told him he could come in, but she hadn't told him he couldn't, either. He trailed her over the grass to the front porch. She remained mute as she unlocked the door, and he followed her inside.

After tossing her jacket onto a hook on the coat tree in the entry hall, Annie glided through a compact living room to the kitchen at the rear of the house. The first thing to catch Keith's eye was the array of tiny stained-glass ornaments dangling in front of the window above the sink: a flower, a crescent moon, a butterfly, an eight-pointed star, a small, semicircular rainbow. The early evening sun entered the west-facing window and passed through the stained glass to cast colorful shapes onto the opposite wall above the kitchen table.

"These are nice," Keith observed, crossing over to the window to examine them more closely. "Where did you get them?"

Rolling up her sleeves, Annie said, "I made them."

Keith stared at her, his eyes lit by a mixture of surprise and admiration. "I didn't know you could do stained glass," he said. For as long as he and Annie had been together, he had never witnessed any artistic tendencies in her.

She shrugged and busied herself with a package of chicken that lay defrosting on a counter near the refrigerator. "When I was staying with Teri in Portland, she introduced me to a friend who ran a crafts school," she explained vaguely.

"Yeah? What else did you learn?"

"Just the stained glass," Annie said laconically. "It was enough."

Enough to divert her, Keith completed the thought. Enough to provide her with a therapeutic outlet for her battered emotions. Enough to distract her from thoughts about Adam. Maybe making stained-glass ornaments had been more creative than bumming around the western half of the country, living from meal to meal, but its purpose was the same: to help a person forget.

Abandoning the window, he moved to one of the chairs by the table and sat. He watched Annie arrange pieces of chicken on a broiler pan and sprinkle spices over them. She slid the pan into the oven and prepared a pot of rice. More rice than she could eat alone, Keith noted. More chicken than she could eat alone. He would rather have taken her out to dinner, just to save her the effort of cooking, but if she wound up asking him to share her meal, he wouldn't be disappointed.

Once everything was cooking, she opened the refrigerator, pulled a bottle of beer from a lower shelf and held it up for Keith to see. "Thank you," he said with a nod.

She pulled out a second bottle, removed two glasses from a cabinet and sat at the table facing him. "All right," she said as he twisted the caps off the bottles. "Let's hear about this job."

He tried to interpret her expression, but she was careful to shield her feelings from him. Her eyes were impassive, her lips neither smiling nor frowning, her delicately shaped chin poked slightly forward. Only her hands revealed a hint of her inner turmoil. After pouring some beer into her glass, she fidgeted nervously with the bottle, sliding her fingernails under the soggy label and peeling it away.

"Do you know George McKenna?"

Her eyes grew round and flashed blue at Keith, and then she nodded. "He's a nice man. He rides his bike a lot, instead of driving. His wife always brings their granddaughter to the preschool story hour Wednesday mornings at the library."

"I met him yesterday," Keith told her. "I met his wife, too. McKenna's a lawyer, you know."

Annie nodded.

"I took a long walk around town yesterday," Keith related, leaning back in his chair and curling his hands around the beer bottle. "While I was walking, I saw a wonderful old brick house, a big, symmetrical colonial with a side entrance and a little sign reading, 'George McKenna, Attorney at Law.' The guy runs his practice right out of his house. I can't remember the last time I saw something like that, Annie. I thought the idea of running a law practice in your own home was extinct.''

"Maybe George McKenna's a dinosaur," Annie proposed wryly.

Keith grinned. "He's not that old, Annie," he joked. "He's still got enough energy to rake his own leaves. I was staring at his house when McKenna came marching out of his garage, dragging a rake. The guy isn't a dinosaur, but he's no spring chicken, either. So I offered to help him.''

"You?" Annie snorted. "Rake leaves?''

"Why not?''

"You live in L.A.," she pointed out. "They don't even have leaves in L.A., let alone leaves that fall off trees.''

"Somehow, even without much previous experience, I figured out how to use a rake." Keith drank some beer, taking the time to gauge Annie's negative attitude. She hadn't even heard the whole story and already she seemed antagonistic toward Keith's plan. He tried to guess the best way to win her over, then decided simply to plow ahead. He'd worry about gaining her support later. "He's been thinking about retiring.''

"Who? George McKenna?''

"That's right. But before he retires, he wants to find someone to take over his practice. It's not that there aren't any other lawyers living in Brenton, but they're all employed by firms up in Hartford, or in Meriden. None of them wants to take over a local practice that entails wills and deeds and an occasional insurance claim. According to McKenna, they're all after the big bucks an attorney can earn at a large firm.''

"Like you," Annie commented before sipping from her glass of beer.

Keith watched her close her lips over the rim of her glass. When she lowered her glass, a thin layer of foam coated her upper lip and she ran the tip of her tongue over it. Keith recalled the way her lips and tongue had felt against his, and he sighed. No use thinking about that now. Annie was obviously not feeling the least bit receptive to him.

"I went after the big bucks," he admitted, accepting her accusation without rancor. "I did a lot of things that weren't right for me. That doesn't mean I have to keep doing them. McKenna's practice is just the sort of thing I've always wanted to do—low key, down to earth, one-on-one, person to person. Helping my neighbors—"

"Your neighbors?" Annie interrupted. "Aren't you jumping the gun?"

"Well, I wouldn't be able to take over McKenna's practice unless I moved to Brenton," Keith logically pointed out. "That's what I'm planning. I'm pretty sure Connecticut and California have a reciprocal bar agreement, so I could be licensed to practice here without too much hassle. And it isn't like McKenna's not earning anything at all—his practice brings in less than I'm making now, but plenty enough to live comfortably."

"Wait a minute." Annie held up her hand and shook her head, justifiably skeptical. "You expect me to believe that all you did was rake George McKenna's leaves for him, and he's ready to hand over his practice to you?"

"Of course not," Keith corrected her. "We raked the leaves and talked for a while, and then we went inside to his den, where he poured us a couple of whiskeys and we talked some more. His wife came in, checked me out, and warned me that Brenton would bore me to tears. I told her that being bored to tears was exactly what I wanted."

Annie shook her head again, but Keith detected no scorn in the gesture. She stood, crossed over to the refrigerator, and began assembling ingredients for a salad. Evidently, she was uneasy about what Keith had told her. He wasn't sure why. He wished she would tell him so he wouldn't have to make assumptions.

She didn't say anything, though. She shredded the lettuce into a bowl, then hacked at the tomato with a large knife, splattering red juice and seeds across the counter. She kept her back to him and bowed her head over her work.

"Damn it," he muttered when her silence extended beyond several minutes. "Tell me, Annie. What's got you so ticked off?"

"What makes you think I'm ticked off?" Annie asked in a taut voice as she furiously chopped a stalk of celery.

"You're mutilating your vegetables," he answered.

She turned on him. "You've been here for all of three days," she said, gesticulating with her knife in an absent-minded way. Keith tried to calculate the odds of her accidentally stabbing him. "All of a sudden you're ready to set up shop in Brenton?"

"How long did you stay in Brenton before you accepted the library job?" Keith asked.

Annie hesitated, then turned away, sparing his life for the moment. "That was different," she mumbled. "I didn't have another job at the time. Anyone who offered me a decent position in a library could have had me. I would have moved anywhere."

"But you moved here, and you stayed," Keith observed. "It's a beautiful town. What's wrong with my wanting to stay, too?"

Once again she lapsed into a tense silence.

"True confessions, Annie," he coaxed her.

She set down her knife, dried her hands on a towel, and turned to him. "Forgive the cliché, Keith, but I think that maybe this town isn't big enough for the two of us."

He digested her words and the blunt message they contained. She didn't want him around. She wanted him gone, as far away as possible. He didn't blame her, but . . . Damn. Couldn't she understand how it could be, if only they gave themselves another chance?

The possibility of buying out George McKenna's small-town law practice had enormous appeal to Keith, but it was only one reason he wanted to stay. Before he'd arrived in Brenton, he had believed that all he wanted was to apologize to Annie, to try to put the past to rest. But ever since he'd seen her, he hadn't been thinking about the past at all. For the first time in ages, he was thinking about the future.

He was tired of merely existing. He wanted to live, to make plans, to do the kind of work that brought him joy, to feel a wild craving for another human being. He'd felt it years ago, with Annie—and he'd felt it again Saturday night. With Annie.

Given her mood at the moment, Keith didn't have much hope of convincing Annie that they could learn to love each other again. If he mentioned the possibility, she'd dispute with him, and love wasn't the sort of thing people ought to debate over. It was something you had to feel in your gut. If Annie didn't feel it, no amount of persuasion on his part would make a difference.

But she couldn't keep him away. Regardless of how small Brenton was, she couldn't prevent him from taking up residence here. "McKenna and I have a lot more talking to do," he said quietly. "He hasn't even set a price on his practice, and he doesn't have anything but my word to go on about my professional background. We have a lot of negotiating to do. But I'm optimistic that we'll be able to work something out. It's what I want, Annie."

"Is it?" she asked caustically. "You've spent all your life dreaming of writing wills in a stagnant town in central Connecticut? Well, that's just swell, Keith. But you'd better not expect me to be driving the Welcome Wagon. I don't want you here. I've been very happy without you in my life."

Keith pressed his lips together to keep from spitting out an equally nasty remark. He turned away from Annie to stare at the ethereal splashes of stained-glass color on the wall. He was hurt by what Annie had said, but more than that he was perplexed. He had never heard her speak so spitefully before, not even when he'd told her he was leaving her.

It was her uncharacteristic bitterness that baffled him. He knew she was behaving this way to mask her own pain. If his leaving hadn't caused her this much pain, why should his return?

He twisted back to her and found her facing the window, leaning her hands against the counter so that her arms were propping her up. Her shoulders trembled almost imperceptibly beneath her shirt.

He stood, took a cautious step toward her, and ran his hand consolingly over her hair. At his touch she flinched, and he pulled his hand away. "Annie," he murmured.

"I don't want you here," she whispered hoarsely, still refusing to look at him.

He exhaled. "There isn't a hell of a lot you can do about it," he remarked gently. "I'm going to stay. So...please try to get used to it."

Getting used to it would take time, he acknowledged silently. But Annie would have that time. An agreement between George McKenna and Keith was far from certain, and even if they were able to hammer out a fair arrangement, Keith would have numerous details to take care of in Los Angeles before he could transplant himself in Connecticut.

Annie would have plenty of time, he conceded as he gazed at the inviting golden river of hair spilling down her back. Indeed, she would have enough time to escape from Brenton before he could settle in. And then he'd have to spend the next lord-knew-how-many years hunting for her again.

He would do it, too. If Annie ever disappeared on him again, he would do whatever it took to find her. Despite her coldness, despite her refusal to turn to him, to smile at him and welcome him back into her world, Keith didn't regret for an instant the fact that he'd struggled so hard to find her.

Two hours later, Annie wrapped her plate of uneaten chicken in aluminum foil and slid it onto a shelf of her refrigerator. She dumped the rice into the trash. She'd made too much rice, anyway. With the chicken, she'd cooked the entire amount in the expectation that it would provide her with several dinners. But as for the rice, there had been no good reason for her to cook a double portion. The only explanation she could think of was that, subconsciously, she had wanted Keith to stay for dinner. And that wasn't a good reason at all.

She was still reeling from his news. The notion of Keith living in the same town, shopping at the same stores, borrowing his books from the Brenton Public Library... What on earth could he be thinking?

Sure, Brenton was a lovely town. Sure, Keith would enjoy the sort of legal practice George McKenna conducted. More than enjoy it—he would do a fine job. Annie remembered the way he'd thrived professionally when they'd lived in Orland. She remembered how devoted he'd been to his clients, how absorbed he'd been by the human dimensions of such a practice. His expensive watch and stylish clothes notwithstanding, she couldn't picture Keith working in a high-power law factory, running up billable hours on behalf of questionable litigants. Apparently, Keith didn't like to picture himself in such an environment, either. He was ready to resume the kind of work he loved.

Fine. Let him work at any job he wanted. But not here, not in Brenton.

Annie wrung out the sponge, set it on the edge of the sink and checked her wristwatch. Eight-thirty. There was a slim chance that Teri would be home from work by now—if she wasn't gallivanting around Portland with her beloved oral surgeon. Annie was desperate to talk to her sister. She left the kitchen for her bedroom, flopped onto the bed, and dialed Teri's number.

This time, thank goodness, Teri was home when Annie needed her. "Hello?"

"Teri? It's Annie."

"Annie!" Teri sounded delighted to hear from her sister, and then suddenly apprehensive when she said, "Two calls in two days makes me nervous, Annie. Please don't tell me it's Keith."

"It's Keith," Annie told her.

"That bastard," Teri muttered. "Is he still in Brenton?"

"Worse than that," Annie lamented. "He says he wants to move here."

Teri took a moment to digest Annie's announcement. "Move there? Like, take a job in town, and *move* there?"

"Yeah."

"That bastard," Teri repeated. "Why? Does he want to torture you some more? Didn't he do enough damage six years ago?"

Annie hesitated. Her heart told her that Keith's motive wasn't to torture her, just as he hadn't intended to hurt her six years ago. He might have acted selfishly then, but it hadn't been a deliberate act to wound Annie.

His claim that he now wanted to move to Brenton wasn't a deliberate act to wound her, either. Once again, it was selfish—he was eager to find his own happiness, regardless of how his choices might affect Annie. At its worst it was selfish, perhaps a little reckless—but at its best... "I think he wants to get back together with me," Annie heard herself declare.

"What?" Teri shrieked.

Annie shook her head. "I don't know why I just said that. Forget it, Teri."

"No, come on," Teri prodded her. "What makes you think he wants to get back together with you? Has he made a pass at you or something?"

"No," Annie said automatically. She didn't like lying to Teri, but she wasn't about to reveal to her sister that Keith had kissed her a couple of nights ago, and that his kiss had disturbed her—that days later, merely thinking about it disturbed her. She wasn't about to tell Teri that she found Keith incredibly sexy. How, after all, could a woman consider a man sexy when that man had caused her so much misery?

"Well, just because he makes a play for you doesn't mean you have to fall for it," Teri advised. "You can thumb your nose at him. You're strong, you don't need him. Now, maybe, it's your turn to break his heart."

Annie was appalled by Teri's suggestion, but she kept her opinion to herself. After they'd briefly discussed Teri's love life, and the dinner party she was arranging to introduce their parents to Craig, Annie hung up. She reconsidered Teri's idea about breaking Keith's heart, and found it just as appalling.

Regardless of how they'd parted, and how long they'd been apart, there was simply no room for deception and game playing in Annie and Keith's relationship. They'd never done it—neither of them liked those sorts of games or were any good at them. Keith might have broken Annie's heart, but it wasn't anything he'd wished for or plotted. He'd acted honestly, and she'd reacted honestly. He'd hurt her and she'd been hurt. Period.

Closing her eyes, she sank her head into the pillow and tried to imagine what her life would be like with Keith in Brenton. She tried to picture herself running into him on the town green, greeting him and chatting about the weather, but she couldn't. She tried to picture him rising to speak out against zoning proposals at the town meetings—and that picture led to one of him getting elected to the representative town council. Annie just knew that if Keith moved to Brenton, he'd have the town fawning all over him in a matter of months.

Not just the town, Annie amended. Women, too. Annie couldn't keep Keith out of Brenton—as he'd reminded her, there wasn't a hell of a lot she could do about his decision to move here. If her intuition was correct, if he wanted to begin a new romance with her, she could reject him, but then he'd likely date other women in town. Forget chatting about the weather with him on the town green—what would it be like to run into him when he was with another woman? What would Annie say when she saw him holding another woman's hand, and gazing adoringly at her, and kissing her cheek?

Keith was a handsome, virile man. If Annie turned him down, he'd find someone else. And it would happen within her town, before her eyes.

He'd dated other women since their breakup; he'd told her as much on Saturday night. What she hadn't known hadn't bothered her, and for the past six years she hadn't known what he'd been doing three thousand miles away. But learning about it *had* bothered her. And having Keith pursue a love life in Brenton would bother her even more.

Unless, of course, she became his love life. Unless hers was the only love he pursued.

But she didn't want that, she decided, opening her eyes and pushing herself to sit. She swung her legs off the bed, stood, and undressed for a shower. The pounding spray of the hot water helped to clear her head, reminding her that, given her past with Keith, she'd have to be a fool to embark on a new relationship with him.

She'd been deeply in love once, and she'd lost everything—her child, her man, her faith in the power of love itself. To let Keith back into her heart would be to set herself up for another loss.

Annie wasn't a fool.

"'But all of a sudden,'" Annie read, "'the clock began to strike twelve. And Cinderella broke from the handsome prince and raced away, knowing that at midnight the spell would be broken. As she ran down the stairs and away from the palace, one of her dainty glass slippers fell off her foot.'"

"Uh-oh!" one of the children blurted out. Annie and the others laughed.

She turned the page and lifted the book high so that all the children could see the colorful illustrations in this large-format edition of *Cinderella*. It was Wednesday morning, and she was hosting her weekly story hour for preschool children. She sat on her swivel chair, which she'd wheeled out from behind the counter and brought to the play corner, and the children sat cross-legged on the floor in front of her. At least most of them did. A couple of them had strayed from the group and were playing with some toy dump trucks they'd found on one of the shelves.

Annie hadn't heard from Keith since he'd left her house Monday night, and her anxiety was beginning to ebb. As positive as he'd sounded when he'd explained his plans to her, she wouldn't be terribly surprised if he didn't follow through with them. Although Keith was a bright, sensible man, he sometimes got caught up in his impulses. In the years after Adam's death, Annie had often pondered the possibility that Keith hadn't been as eager to have a child as

Annie had, but that he'd simply been swept up by her enthusiasm. Maybe he hadn't been as enthralled as she had been by living in Orland, either—if he had been, he wouldn't have moved away. Maybe he'd simply agreed to move to the farming community with her on another impulse. If a place or an idea struck him as interesting, he plunged in with all his energy. But then, once the novelty wore off, he stepped back, distanced himself, rethought the impulse.

When Keith failed to contact Annie all day Tuesday, she found herself hoping that moving to Brenton might be another impulsive notion Keith had chosen to reconsider.

"'...And the prince traveled throughout the town, searching for the woman who had worn the glass slipper. He was desperately in love with the beautiful woman with whom he had danced at the ball, and he wanted to marry her and bring her back to the castle to live with him. The only way to find this woman was to find out who could fit the tiny, dainty slipper onto her foot.'"

Cinderella wasn't much like "Sophie the Dragon" or any of the other stories Annie had made up for the entertainment of the children at Shandler's Family Day promotion. But the children loved classic fairy tales, so Annie indulged them. They listened quietly as she read page after page, displaying illustration after illustration. "'And as soon as he slipped the shoe onto Cinderella's foot, he gazed up into her eyes and knew that she was the woman he had lost his heart to at the ball. She was the woman he wanted for his wife. And so he took her back to the castle with him and they lived happily ever after.'"

"If the shoe fits, wear it!" came a sweet, high-pitched voice from the center of the crowd of children. Annie quickly located its source: Jennifer Harper, the youngest daughter of Steve Harper, Annie's one-time suitor. Given that her father was extremely bright and literate, and that she had two older siblings, Jennifer tended to be precocious. As soon as Annie caught the little girl's eye, Jennifer grinned bashfully and said, "That's a 'spression."

"And a particularly apt one," Annie complimented her. "Okay, kids, that was the last story for today. You can look at books by yourselves until someone comes to pick you up." The children were too young to leave the library alone, but the parents or guardians who had brought them to the story hour knew when it ended and usually showed up promptly to escort the children home. Annie knew that many of the parents took advantage of the story hours to browse upstairs in the adult section of the library.

Steve Harper wasn't upstairs; he was down the street running his bookstore. In five minutes he would be taking his lunch break, and he'd pick Jennifer up then. Even after he and Annie had stopped dating, they'd remained good friends, and she knew his routines.

Jennifer and the other children dispersed, some to flip through the oversize picture books Annie had left on the tables and some to play with the available toys. Adults— mostly mothers—started trooping down the stairs to collect their children.

Among the adults Annie spotted a petite woman in her early sixties, with short gray hair and a figure that still looked smart in a pair of designer jeans. Annie recognized her: George McKenna's wife, Beatrice, coming to pick up their granddaughter. Beatrice took care of Erica while Erica's parents worked as accountants in Meriden. Brenton was too small to offer much in the way of formal day care for the children of working mothers, but it was such a family-oriented town that, in many cases, several generations of the same family lived close by and helped each other out. Jennifer Harper spent most of her daytime hours with Steve's in-laws. Beatrice McKenna baby-sat for Erica. It was simply the way things were done in Brenton.

Beatrice waved at Annie before wading into the mob of children to fetch Erica. Annie smiled and waved back, and watched as Beatrice wrapped her hands around Erica's waist and plucked her off the floor. "Time for lunchie-munchkins," Beatrice singsonged. She was a grandmother, so Annie forgave her her corniness.

Annie and Beatrice exchanged waves and smiles again as Beatrice and Erica passed the counter and headed for the stairs. As soon as they were gone, Annie felt her shoulders slump and she dropped weakly onto the chair. She hadn't realized until that moment how anxious she was about the status of Keith and George's negotiations. She hadn't realized how tempted she'd been to ask Beatrice what was going on between her husband and Keith.

Annie didn't want to care. She didn't even want to believe that Keith was serious about staying in Brenton. But she knew, deep down, that he was serious, and that she cared very, very much.

The door at the top of the stairs swung open again, and Steve Harper entered. Familiar with the children's library, he remembered to duck as he bounded down the stairs. He headed straight for the counter. "Hello, Annie," he hailed her, his voice soft but spirited. "How's my favorite competitor doing?"

Annie grinned. Steve frequently teased her about how the library ate into his book sales. "Business is lively," she reported. "How are things down the road?"

"Pulling out of the end-of-summer slump, gearing up for the Christmas boom. Where's my lunch date?"

Annie stood and nodded toward the play corner, where Jennifer was ensconced. Before Steve left the counter, Annie quickly filled him in on his daughter's witty summation of Cinderella. Steve laughed appreciatively, then bade Annie goodbye and went to get his daughter.

Steve was a pleasant-looking man with large features and a natural smile. Annie found him attractive, even now, when their failed romance was years in the past. She wondered fleetingly whether, if Keith moved to Brenton and dated other women, she could start dating Steve again.

No, she couldn't. For one thing, she treasured her friendship with Steve, and dating him would jeopardize it. For another, she would never use anyone—not to make Keith jealous and not to balance some imaginary scale.

For another, she wasn't going to play that sort of game.

Steve called another farewell to Annie as he and Jennifer ascended the stairs and left the library. Although they were poorly matched as lovers, Annie had truly liked dating Steve. She had liked the lack of pressure, the feeling of control she'd had with him. Unlike the kiss she'd shared with Keith, there was nothing about Steve that could sweep Annie away, but she had liked the safety and security he represented. She had also liked Steve's willingness to let his emotions show. He had suffered a terrible loss when his wife had died, but unlike Keith, he hadn't dealt with it by running away. Steve had faced his grief with dignity.

Annie had never known Steve's wife, but in a perverse way she could identify with the woman. Not because she had briefly dated Steve, but because, like his deceased wife, Annie had been deprived of the joy of seeing her child grow up. In the case of Steve's wife, though, things had occurred in the right order. What great thinker had said that for a parent to bury a child was the cruelest fate?

Why was she thinking such things? Annie blinked the tears from her eyes and forced a limp smile and a wave for the remaining children and their mothers. Once the children's library was empty, she lowered herself onto her chair and rested her head on top of her folded arms on the counter. A few more tears leaked through her lashes and she sniffled them away.

It was all Keith's fault—dredging up the memories, bringing back to life the bitterness she had worked so hard to conquer. She hated being this way—melancholy, maudlin, teetering on the edge of depression. She hadn't been this disconsolate in years, but now Keith had come and brought too many agonizing memories with him.

His departure had caused her pain. His return was causing her even more pain. And she felt helpless to do anything but pray that he'd leave again.

Five

—

He kept his distance from Annie. He didn't want her feeling crowded or pressured—at least not any more crowded or pressured than she already felt.

She'd reacted badly to the news of his decision to move to Brenton. He had entertained the hope—a groundless hope, he acknowledged—that she'd be delighted to have him back in her life. Far from delighted, she'd seemed horrified.

Time was supposed to heal wounds, yet wounds that appeared healthy sometimes twinged with pain long after the fact, if the conditions were right. As a teenager, Keith had broken his ankle during a soccer game. The bones had mended perfectly; he had regained complete mobility in his foot, and within a year he'd lost his limp. But to this day, his mended, healthy ankle was more accurate than the National Weather Service at predicting a change in the humidity. The minute a chilly wet front approached, the scar tissue in his ankle joint throbbed.

Annie might be strong, but she had scars, too, scars that ached at the first sign of a storm. And, unlike a storm, Keith wasn't going to make her uncomfortable for a few days and then blow out to sea. He was going to stay.

In time Annie would understand that he wasn't a storm, hovering over her world with the sole purpose of tormenting her. In time—in not too much time, he prayed—she would admit what Keith already recognized: that the worst mistake they'd ever made in their lives was to withdraw from each other when they ought to have reached out and leaned on each other. Just because they'd failed each other six years ago didn't mean they had to fail now.

If he steered clear of her for a while, maybe she would recognize that truth, too. He'd give her as much time as he could, and hope it was all the time she would need.

All of which didn't mean he couldn't see her, though. It didn't mean he couldn't drive past her house at night in order to glimpse her silhouette against the closed drapes of her living-room window. It didn't mean he couldn't park across the green from the library at a few minutes to five and watch her exit the building and lock the children's library entrance, then turn up the collar of her jacket as the evening wind whipped her streaming golden hair back from her face. It didn't mean he couldn't spy on her at midday, when she strolled down the sidewalk bordering the green during her lunch break, window-shopping in the stores or dropping a letter into the mailbox outside the post office.

Of course, most of Keith's time was spent with George McKenna, comparing legal philosophies and courtroom strategies, figuring out schedules and discussing ethics. And talking money—the value of McKenna's client lists, the value of his law library, Keith's ability and willingness to pay what McKenna believed the entire practice was worth. There was a great deal of haggling, but it was friendly haggling.

Keith liked McKenna. The old man was both compassionate and shrewd, unlike most of the senior partners at Keith's firm in Los Angeles, who were shrewd but lacking in heart. Keith's father was like them—clever, brilliant at manipulating people and achieving his ends, but not terribly sensitive. He was a successful businessman, and while he'd been proud of his son for attending law school, he'd been aghast when Keith had taken his law degree to Orland to offer his services to the farm laborers. Keith's father was happy with Keith's current job, but Keith wasn't living his life to make his father happy. He much preferred McKenna's sense of humanity to his father's business acumen.

Not matter how much time Keith spent with George McKenna, however, thoughts of Annie were never far away. Keith might be sitting in McKenna's office, listening to McKenna describe the damage claims he'd handled in the past eight months or the local zoning proposals for which he'd filed amicus curae briefs, and suddenly an image of Annie would flash across Keith's mind: a picture of her leaving the library with that little girl, Justine, clinging to her hand; a picture of her in her slim-fitting green knit dress, circling her arms around him and parting her lips as he bent to kiss her; a picture of her in her kitchen, with her back to him and her head bowed as she whispered, "I don't want you here."

It was probably crazy, pulling up stakes and journeying across the country just to be with a woman who didn't even want him. But Keith was convinced that staying away from Annie would be even crazier.

He hoped with all his might that she'd soon be convinced of it, too.

"I've got to go back to Los Angeles," he said.

Annie sat on the edge of her bed and tightened her grip on the telephone receiver. Nine days had elapsed since Keith had wheedled his way into her house and informed her that he was planning to relocate to Brenton—nine days during which she'd heard nothing at all from him. At times, she had thought she spotted him behind the wheel of a familiar-looking Pontiac, which was parked on one of the roads by the green, but he'd never left the car or called to her, and she'd figured that she'd been mistaken.

Since he hadn't phoned her, either, she had begun to wonder whether he'd taken her sentiments to heart and permanently departed from Brenton. If that were the case, she would have thought he'd contact her to let her know he was leaving. Maybe that was what this call was about.

She assessed his announcement and wondered why she didn't feel cheerful about it. "When are you going?" she asked.

"Tomorrow. I might be there for a month or two, Annie. I've got a lot of business to take care of."

Then he wasn't leaving for good. That comprehension didn't cheer her, either.

"Annie," he went on when she didn't speak, "I know you've got mixed emotions about all this—"

"Who says they're mixed?" she countered. They *were* mixed, but he didn't have to know that.

Keith hesitated, then pushed ahead. "I've been spending the past week working out the details with McKenna. He wants to cut back gradually, to make his retirement as smooth as possible. So we're probably going to form a temporary partnership, which will allow me to buy him out slowly. He's drawing up the contracts now. In the meantime, I've got to serve notice at the firm in L.A., and see about subletting my apartment—"

"Keith," she cut him off. "Keith, why are you telling me this? You know how I feel about it."

"No," he said, his tone quiet but pointed. "I don't know." He paused, then added, "I don't think you do, either."

"Would you like me to spell it out?"

"No," he said quickly. "What I'd like is to see you." As if he could sense the refusal taking shape on her tongue, he hastily added, "I've stayed away from you all this time, Annie. I've done my best to respect your feelings—whatever they are. Show a little respect for me, Annie. Let me see you before I leave."

"What for?" she asked, sounding more bewildered than resistant. "If you want a romantic farewell—"

"That's not what I want," Keith insisted, then issued a wistful laugh. "Actually, it's exactly what I want, but I'm not counting on it. Annie, I just want to see you. I want to prepare myself for what I'll be coming back to when I return to Connecticut."

Annie took a minute to decipher his comment. Something about it implied that if he didn't see her, if he didn't get the romantic farewell he wanted, if she didn't give him a chance to prepare himself, his resolution might falter. If she forced him to accept the absolute fact that she didn't want him in her life, he might just give up and leave her alone.

She couldn't rid herself of the suspicion that Keith was simply caught up in something he hadn't really thought through. If she saw him, she'd be encouraging his delusion. If she didn't see him, he'd face reality and let go.

"I'm sorry," she said, surprised by the genuine emotion her statement carried. "I'm sorry, Keith, but no. I can't see you tonight."

He was silent for a moment. Then he spoke, a single word, hushed yet intense: "Please."

"No."

Another silence. "All right," he said, his tone subdued. "All right, Annie. I'll go without saying goodbye. Maybe that's for the best. I don't really want to say goodbye to you."

She smothered the urge to ask him when he was planning to return. "Then we won't say goodbye," she agreed, trying to ignore the heavy sense of doubt closing in on her. This was for the best. They didn't need to say goodbye; they didn't need to put their parting into words. Just as long as Keith left, as long as he freed her to live the rest of her life in peace.

The metallic click inside the receiver jolted her. It was followed by a second click, and then the steady purr of the dial tone. Keith had hung up.

She set the receiver down in its cradle and shook her head. Was he actually gone? Was this truly the end?

She stood and wandered to the kitchen, where she'd been fixing herself a sandwich. Her appetite had vanished, and after staring at her plate for fifteen minutes she threw the food away. Then she roamed into her living room, flopped onto the sofa, gazed at the blank television set and meditated.

She was testing Keith, and she didn't like it. Her refusal to see him before he left was simply her way of testing his resolve, trying to measure how serious he was about returning. They'd had their arguments in the past, they'd had their spats and their disagreements, but they'd never tested each other this way. She couldn't do it now.

She had to be honest with him. She had to see him and tell him, one last time, that she didn't want him in Brenton. To do less would be dishonest. Keith had asked for her respect; she owed him that much.

Sighing, she walked back to the bedroom. She pulled the telephone directory from her night table shelf, thumbed through it until she found the number of the Brenton Motor

Inn, and dialed. When the desk clerk answered, Annie requested Keith LaMotte's room.

It rang. And rang again. Twelve times. Annie hung up.

Maybe he was in the hotel's restaurant. Maybe he was spending the evening with George McKenna. Maybe he was loitering on the green, or downing a stiff drink at Riley's.

Earlier, she'd been sure that she mustn't see him. Now she was sure that she had to. The clerk hadn't said anything about Keith checking out, so wherever he'd disappeared to, eventually he'd have to go back to the motel. Annie ran her hairbrush through her hair, smoothed her pleated corduroy slacks beneath the ribbed edge of her sweater, scooped up her keys and purse from the top of the dresser and left the house. She would go to the motel, and if he was out she'd wait for him.

She arrived at the motel ten minutes later. The rental car Keith had been using was parked in the lot. Annie inhaled deeply, then strode inside the motel lobby, heading straight for the desk. "Could you ring Keith LaMotte's room, please?" she asked the clerk. "Tell him Annie Jameson is here to see him."

The clerk nodded and lifted his switchboard phone. While a part of Annie's attention was focused on him, listening to him announce her arrival, another part of her attention was directed inward to the tangled knot of emotion weighing down her heart.

What was she going to say to Keith when she saw him? What if, after she stated, plainly and firmly, that she did not want him to return to Brenton, he shrugged and said, "I'm going after McKenna's practice, and tough luck to you?"

What if, even worse, he repeated his comment about desiring a "romantic farewell"? What if he tried to kiss her? What if he kissed her the way he had outside the restaurant on Saturday night over a week ago, and she responded the way she had, and she temporarily forgot how much she wanted him gone? What if—

"He said you should come to his room," the clerk reported, lowering his intercom phone. "It's room one-eighteen. Down the hall on your left."

Annie nodded and marched with false bravery to the hall. Once she was beyond the clerk's range of vision she halted and took another deep breath, wishing with all her might that it would clear her mind.

His room. Why on earth was she going to his room? She'd never been in a motel room with a man before!

A nervous laugh escaped her. For heaven's sake, this wasn't a man—it was Keith. Her one-time lover, her one-time best friend. The man she'd lived with, the father of her son. She didn't have to act like a skittish virgin. This was *Keith*. No matter how much bad blood had spilled between them, she trusted him. And she trusted herself with him.

Bolstered by her silent pep talk, she straightened her shoulders and stalked down the hall to room 118. She knocked on the door, and it swung open instantly.

This was Keith, all right—only it was Keith half-naked, his bronze skin shimmering with moisture, his chest and arms exposed to Annie's startled eyes. His hair was wet, too, and uncombed, and he had a bath towel slung around his neck. He was wearing jeans and his feet were bare. His smile was wide, gloriously bright, and punctuated with dimples. "Annie! You're here!"

She saw him reaching for her arm, and she quickly stepped across the threshold, eluding him. The sight of his body was disconcerting enough; if he touched her, she'd be even more disconcerted.

He closed the door behind her and gestured toward the one chair in the room, a clunky-looking armchair upholstered in brown Naugahyde. A leather suitcase, which lay open on the circular pedestal table next to the chair, had a few items in it. A briefcase stood on the floor between the chair and the double bed.

"Sit down," Keith invited her, as he glided across the room to switch on the table lamp. "I just got out of the shower—as you probably guessed. Give me a minute to brush my hair and shave—"

"You don't have to shave," Annie said, crossing the room to sit. She was reassured by her smooth, light tone.

His smile grew gentle as he peered down at her. "I do have to comb my hair," he said, lifting the towel from his shoulders and running it over his dripping dark hair. He slung the towel onto the knob of the bathroom door, then moved to the dresser, lifted his brush and neatened his hair.

Annie tried not to ogle him, but she couldn't help herself. From where she sat, she had a magnificent view of his back with its lean, tapering stretch of muscle beneath sundarkened skin. His shoulders were as broad and bony as she'd remembered, and his arms were still strong and sinewy, covered by a silky webbing of dark hair. She was also able to see his reflection in the mirror—a reflection of his well-shaped chest, enhanced by a sparse adornment of hair, his flat, sleek abdomen, the sexy indentation of his navel a couple of inches above the low-slung waistband of his jeans...

She quickly forced her gaze upward to concentrate on his jaw. He'd sprouted a faint day-old bristle, but she saw no need for him to shave. He hated shaving—at least he used to hate it six years ago.

"You should have called me and given me some warning," he reproached her, parting his hair and slicking it back from his forehead.

"I did," Annie told him. "About fifteen minutes ago. You didn't answer the phone."

"Funny thing about that," Keith said with a chuckle. "I was in the shower." He placed his brush on the dresser and rotated back to her. "I'm so glad you came, Annie," he murmured. "I really didn't want to have to leave without seeing you."

Annie wasn't ready yet to talk about how glad Keith was that she'd come, or about how glad she was that he was leaving. Instead, she said, "You must spend a lot of time in the sun."

As soon as the words slipped out she regretted them. They revealed to Keith how closely she'd inspected his body.

He shrugged, evidently unconcerned about the implications of her remark. "There's a swimming pool in the apartment complex where I live," he informed her. "I swim laps three or four times a week."

That not only explained his tan but also the excellent shape he was in. The first summer they'd lived in Orland, she and Keith had donned swimsuits, filled two inner tubes with air and floated down the Sacramento River. Tubing on the river had been a popular sport in the Sacramento Valley. But it wasn't the same thing as swimming laps. Annie tried to envision Keith in a swimsuit now, his thighs and calves honed to athletic perfection, his powerful arms slicing through the water.

She closed her eyes to erase the image. Silently, she repeated the pep talk she'd given herself out in the corridor. This was Keith. A man she'd once loved, a man she'd once hated. A man to whom she'd come to say goodbye.

"I came to say goodbye," she announced, opening her eyes.

Keith had reached for a shirt. His fingers tightened around the white cotton fabric as he narrowed his gaze on Annie. Then he relaxed and slid his arms through the sleeves. "How about some dinner?" he suggested, as if she hadn't even spoken.

"I already ate," she fibbed, then chastised herself. She had come here with the intention of being totally honest with

Keith. She wasn't going to lie to him, not even about her appetite. "No, Keith, I didn't eat. I fixed myself a sandwich, but I wound up throwing it out."

An undefinable emotion flickered across his face. Leaving his shirt unbuttoned, he crossed to the bed and sat on it, facing Annie, inches from her. "You want to know the truth?" he confessed, a sheepish smile teasing his lips. "I went down the hall to the restaurant, ordered a hamburger, and didn't eat a bite."

She wasn't sure what to make of his admission. That Keith was suffering from as much emotional turmoil as she was astonished her—yet why should it? He was a human being, too. Surely this entire episode—his search for Annie, his confronting her, his decision to take up residence in her town—was as unsettling to him as it was to her.

"You must be starving," she said, feeling the corners of her mouth twitch upward. Lord, but it felt good to share her nervousness with Keith, to smile with him, to feel friendly toward him again.

He shook his head. "No," he swore. "Anyway, I want to save myself for the delicious meal they're sure to serve on the airplane tomorrow."

"You're really leaving?" she asked, anxious for confirmation. "You're really going back to California?"

"For a while."

"Keith." Her smile faded as she reminded herself of her purpose in rushing to the motel tonight. "I came here, Keith, because we do have to say goodbye to each other. I had some silly idea that if I didn't see you before you left, you wouldn't come back—"

"Annie—"

"I know, it was stupid. It was unfair of me. And it probably was wrong. You'll do whatever you want to do, Keith—you always have. You wanted to leave six years ago, and you left. If you want to come back now, you will, whether or not

I say goodbye. But...I'm here to ask you...to beg you...very politely..." Her voice cracked before she could finish, and she averted her eyes.

Keith reached for her, and this time Annie didn't shy away from him. He folded his hands around hers, letting his arms span the space between her knees and his. "No, Annie," he said with quiet determination. He took a moment to mull over his thoughts, then continued, weighing each word before he uttered it. "I've got to go to Los Angeles for a while, and then I'm coming back. I want to be here, with you. I love you, Annie. I did then, and I do now, and I probably did all those years in between. I love you." He let go of her hands, stood and paced for a minute, running his fingers through his damp hair and mussing it. "I wasn't going to talk about this, Annie. I'm so afraid of frightening you. Well, I'm frightened, too. But that doesn't change anything. I want you back."

Stunned, she stared up at him, feeling his words resonate within her. He loved her. He wanted her back. He was frightened, but not so frightened that he didn't have the courage to speak his heart.

"I don't see how that can happen," she mumbled, clinging to her own resolution, willing herself to match Keith in stubbornness. "You left me, Keith—"

"I left you. It was a long time ago. I've grown up, Annie, and so have you. You were the one who said you wanted to let it be. I agree. The past is gone, and we're here."

He sounded as positive as she felt uncertain. She tried to remember how much he'd hurt her, but her memory was overrun by the present, by his intensity and his sincerity. *I'm frightened too,* he had sworn. *But that doesn't change anything. I want you back.*

He loved her. If she were as honest as Keith, she would have to admit that she still loved him, too, that she'd loved him then and she loved him now, and she'd probably loved him in the intervening years, as well. If she didn't love him, his return wouldn't have upset her so much. If she didn't love him, her emotions wouldn't be in such a frenzy.

She peered into his eyes, smoky gray and unwavering on her, and she understood that she had never stopped loving him. Her failure to become involved with another man since Keith had left wasn't a result of the scarcity of single men. It was simply that she couldn't give her heart to someone new when it still belonged to Keith.

She didn't want to love him. It seemed far more reasonable to hate him. But she couldn't deny the truth.

"Oh, Keith." She sighed and looked away. "You're right. You've scared me."

He crossed back to her, hooked his index finger under her chin and lifted her face to his. "Let's be brave together, all right?" he advised, smiling hesitantly. "We'll take it slow, if you want. We don't have to rush into anything—"

"Damn it, Keith, why do you have to be so rational?" Annie flared, then burst into laughter. "What exactly do you have in mind? Are we supposed to go out on dates? Should we go steady? You've just dropped a bomb on me, and now you're telling me you want to take it slow?"

Keith smiled, too, but his smile was dark and sensual. "I don't want to take it slow at all," he murmured, gripping her wrists and hauling her out of the chair. He slid his hands up her arms to her shoulders and pulled her to him. "I love you, Annie," he whispered, dropping a light kiss on the crown of her head. "What do you think I want?"

Annie knew what he wanted. As he tightened his hold on her, as she lifted her hands to his shoulders, as she tilted her head back and offered him her lips, she knew that she wanted the same thing. She wanted to forget the past, to vanquish the hatred, to love Keith the way she had loved him so long ago. She wanted to love him, body and soul, to love him until she was no longer sure where she ended and he began, to love him with a passion that transcended law and ritual and official pieces of paper.

Their lips met. The control she had sensed in Keith the last time he'd kissed her was scarcely in evidence now. Within an instant, he was probing her mouth with his tongue, delving inside, teasing and luring. He cupped the back of her head with one hand and dropped the other to her waist, drawing her even closer.

Perhaps if he were fully clothed, Annie wouldn't have responded so insanely to his kiss. But his shirt hung open, and she was unable to keep her hands off his warm, naked chest. She explored the contoured muscles, the masculine covering of hair, the curved ribs along his sides. When she reached his waist, he pulled his lips from hers and groaned softly.

"Lie down," he implored, his voice hoarse, barely audible. He guided her the short distance to the bed and urged her down onto it, then sprawled out beside her. "Oh, Annie..." The words dissolved into another groan as he bowed to kiss her again. He brushed her lips with short, searing nips, scraping the surface of her chin with his scratchy growth of beard. "Annie, Annie—I can't stop kissing you."

To prove his assertion, he kissed her again, a deep, plundering kiss that brought tears to her eyes. While his lips and tongue performed their magic on her mouth, his hand traveled down to her breast. He traced the soft, round swell through the fabric of her sweater.

She shuddered in response, and his gentle caresses slowly narrowed to center on her nipple, which immediately stiffened and sent a burning message downward, into her belly and below. A hushed moan escaped her, partly delight and partly frustration that his hand wasn't closer, directly on her, skin to skin. He clearly understood her frustration, because he lowered his hand to the edge of the sweater and then slipped beneath it. Stroking upward, he shoved the

Say YES to free gifts worth over $20.00

Say YES to a rendezvous with romance, and you'll get 4 classic love stories—FREE! You'll get an attractive digital quartz clock/calendar—FREE! And you'll get a delightful surprise—FREE! These gifts carry a value of over $20.00—but you can have them without spending even a penny!

FREE HOME DELIVERY

Say YES to Silhouette and you'll enjoy the convenience of previewing 6 brand-new books delivered right to your home every month before they appear in stores. Each book is yours for only $2.24—26¢ less than retail, and there is no extra charge for postage and handling.

SPECIAL EXTRAS—FREE!

You'll get our monthly newsletter, packed with news of your favorite authors and upcoming books— FREE! You'll also get additional free gifts from time to time as a token of our appreciation for being a home subscriber.

Say YES to a Silhouette love affair. Complete, detach and mail your Free Offer Card today!

FREE—COMBINATION CLOCK/CALENDAR.

You'll love your new LCD digital quartz clock, which also shows the current month and date. This lovely lucite piece includes a handy month-at-a-glance calendar, or you can display your favorite photo in the calendar area. This is our special gift to you!

FILL OUT THIS POSTPAID CARD AND MAIL TODAY!

SILHOUETTE BOOKS®

FREE OFFER CARD

4 FREE BOOKS

FREE HOME DELIVERY

Place YES sticker here

FREE CLOCK/ CALENDAR

FREE SURPRISE BONUS

Please send me 4 Silhouette Desire® novels, free, along with my free combination clock/calendar and surprise gift as explained on the opposite page.

225 CIL JAYH

Name _____
(PLEASE PRINT)

Address _____Apt. _____

City _____

State _____Zip _____

Offer limited to one per household and not valid for present Desire subscribers. Prices subject to change.

PRINTED IN U.S.A.

DETACH AND MAIL CARD TODAY

BUSINESS REPLY CARD

First Class   Permit No. 717   Buffalo, NY

Postage will be paid by addressee

RUSH! FREE
GIFTS DEPT.

Silhouette Books®
901 Fuhrmann Blvd.
P.O. Box 1867
Buffalo, New York 14240-9952

NO POSTAGE
NECESSARY
IF MAILED
IN THE
UNITED STATES

cloth out of his way. When he reached her bra, he undid the clasp, then lifted her shoulders high enough to strip off her clothing.

He gazed at her breasts, then touched one gently, following a twisting line with his fingertips before rubbing the flushed nipple with his thumb. "Annie," he whispered breathlessly.

"Why do you keep saying my name?" she asked, transported by the sensations that continued to blaze down from her breast.

"Because I can't believe this is real," he answered, turning his attention to her other breast, treating it to the same divine torture. He bowed to kiss her throat, to nibble at her earlobe. "I can't believe how good this is." His voice was low and potent, entering her ear on a heated breath. "Touch me, Annie. Feel what you're doing to me."

Annie wasn't aware that she'd been doing anything at all, other than lying back and reacting, drowning in the sublime passion Keith had awakened in her. Eager to excite him as he was exciting her, she skimmed her fingers down over his chest to his stomach. His hand arrived first, groping for the button of his jeans and opening it for her. She slid her hand in and encountered the curly nest of hair lurking just beneath the zipper. At her shy touch, he gasped and surged against her.

"That's what you do to me," he moaned, trapping one of her legs between his. "You always have, Annie." He lifted himself onto her and fused his mouth to hers. His chest crushed down onto hers, and he reached for her hips, digging his fingers into her bottom and pressing her to him.

She felt his arousal through the layers of cloth separating them. She felt her own arousal even more keenly, in every nerve in her body, in every cell. Keith had always been able to do this to her, too. He had always made her half crazy with yearning. Even if they'd made love hours earlier, or just minutes, he had always been able to make her long for him again. And now, after so many lonely years without him, she hungered for him even more strongly, more insatiably.

He inched his hand forward, over the rise of her hip bone and down between her thighs. She cried out, arching to him, wishing the remainder of her clothing, and his, would miraculously disappear, allowing their bodies complete contact, complete possession. But instead of removing her slacks or his own, he slid lower on her and covered her breast with his mouth.

She moaned at the tantalizing friction of his lips on her, his tongue, his beard-roughened chin chafing her, his teeth gingerly scraping her swollen nipple, drawing it in, sucking. For a delirious moment, she lost herself in the bliss of it. The last time she'd felt anything this intimate, anything this satisfying had been...six years ago. When she'd nursed Adam.

An abrupt chill swept through her, and she fell back from Keith, sinking deep into the mattress. "No," she moaned, twisting her head to break away from his kiss. "Please stop."

He lifted his head, lifted his body from hers and struggled for a moment with his ragged breath. "Why?" he asked, his voice husky with a gentleness that made Annie's heart turn over. He wasn't angry or impatient. He respected her, even in his disappointment.

Daring to turn back to him, she found his expression tender and concerned as he scrutinized her. It wasn't his fault; he couldn't be blamed for her sudden jitters. She still wanted him, she still loved him. But the thought of Adam, of any baby, of the consequences of what she was doing with Keith...

"I—" She swallowed and fought with her own erratic breath. "I didn't come here expecting this."

He smiled, a sweet, dimpled smile. "I didn't come to Brenton expecting this, Annie," he reminded her. "But—"

"That's not what I meant," she corrected him. A thick lock of his hair flopped down onto his brow, and she brushed it back, allowing her hand to float across his temple. "I meant here, this room, now. I'm not prepared, Keith. I didn't...I didn't bring anything. I can't make love to you."

His breathing grew slower, deeper. She watched the pumping of his chest, then raised her eyes to his face again. His dimples had faded, and his eyes seemed shadowed, inscrutably dark.

He was a grown-up, mature, supposedly responsible. Didn't he understand? "I don't want to get pregnant," she elaborated, furious that she had to put it into words.

He pulled himself completely off her, sat up, bent his knees and rested his forearms across them. "Not with me, anyway," he said in a strained voice. "We certainly wouldn't want that."

What was wrong with him? It wasn't Adam she was talking about—it was simply the practical issue of avoiding an accident. Was Keith's ego so fragile that he couldn't even talk about birth control without taking it personally?

"All I'm saying is, let's be adults, Keith. I think we ought to be careful, and—"

"I agree," he said, his tone clipped and cold. "Let's not take any chances. We could find ourselves with another baby, and then we might lose it and we'll both go off the deep end again." He heaved himself to his feet, buttoned his shirt, tucked in the tails and fastened his jeans. "Do you want to leave?"

She was stunned by the transformation in him. Was this the same man who had been making such spellbinding love to her just minutes ago? How could he have changed from someone so sensitive and passionate to someone seething with barely contained rage?

Rage. Pain. Hatred. Angry emotions emanated from Keith, lacerating Annie. She couldn't believe he'd suffered from Adam's death as much as she had. But he had suffered. "We've got to talk about this," she said quietly, sitting up as well.

He stared at her half-naked body, at the wild tumble of her blond hair, at the lingering blush in her cheeks and the not-yet-extinguished glow of desire in her eyes. A low, anguished sigh tore itself from his throat and he turned away. "I need a drink," he said before leaving the room, slamming the door behind him.

Six

***

Annie stared at the closed door. Her body felt feverish, aching hollowly for the love Keith had promised and failed to give her. Yet her mind focused not on the passion she and Keith had been caught up in but on his swift departure. And his anger.

She wondered when he was coming back. Sooner or later he would have to—he hadn't finished packing yet, and he'd have to settle his motel bill before he left for California. But that didn't mean he wanted Annie to be there when he came back.

The last time he'd run away, he had left her behind in Orland, in the house they'd shared for a year and a half. This time, he had abandoned her in alien territory. Annie surveyed the room, with its nondescript furniture, the trite landscape paintings bolted to the walls, the neutral-colored carpeting and the chart fastened to the back of the door, identifying the building's fire exits. Her vision came to rest on the door itself, the door through which Keith had vanished, the door he'd slammed with violent force.

Slowly, her arms responding sluggishly to the commands of her brain, she twisted around and grasped her bra and sweater. She dressed herself, then stood and moved in a daze to the dresser, where she lifted Keith's hair brush and ran it through the tangles of her hair. She often used to borrow his brush when they were living together, and Keith used to complain about the long blond strands he'd find trapped in the bristles. Annie wondered vaguely whether he'd be irked by her having borrowed his brush tonight.

Once her hair was reasonably neat, she set down the brush and examined her reflection in the mirror. The color in her cheeks was high, and her blue eyes seemed uncommonly bright—not just because of the physical rapture she and Keith had nearly surrendered to, she acknowledged, but because of the strong feelings that existed between them, feelings that had never disappeared and could no longer be ignored.

Strong feelings, yes—but were they love or hate? Or both? With a deep sigh, Annie turned from the mirror and walked to the upholstered chair. Sitting, she stared at the wrinkled bedspread and recalled exactly what had created all those wrinkles. Thinking about how marvelous it had felt to be kissed by Keith, to have his weight on her and his body moving against her caused a sob to fill her throat. She swallowed it back down and batted her eyes until the urge to cry had passed.

What had happened on the bed wasn't as important as what was happening now, she sternly reminded herself. What was happening now was that Keith had fled from Annie and was off somewhere, drinking himself into a stupor. She was horrified by the thought of him tranquilizing himself with liquor. He hadn't been much of a drinker when she'd known him years ago. But he had told her, when they'd gone out to dinner a week ago, that after he had left her he'd been a bum. He had defined a bum as someone who drank too much.

He'd been a bum, he'd drunk too much, he'd had no permanent address...and now, at the mere mention of birth control, he'd run for cover. All because of Adam.

Good lord, how could Annie have been stupid enough to think that Keith had made his peace with the past? How could she and he have gotten this far—her eyes drifted to the messy bed again, and she moaned brokenly—how could they have allowed things to get so heated between them when neither of them had the guts to broach the subject of Adam's death?

It was something they simply had to talk about. Annie arranged herself more comfortably in the chair, determined to wait for Keith's return. Even if he dragged himself back to the room after midnight, singing "How Dry I Am" off-key and garbling the words, she would be there, waiting, ready to talk. They could no longer leave the most important things unsaid.

As it turned out, she didn't have to wait until midnight. Keith let himself back into the room less than fifteen minutes after he'd left, carrying two chilled cans of cola. He tossed the key into an unused ashtray and lifted one of the plastic-wrapped glasses the chambermaid had left on the dresser. Without speaking to Annie, without even looking at her, Keith popped open a can, poured some soda into the glass, and carried it across the room to her. Only as he handed it to her did he allow his eyes to graze her face. He smiled pensively, briefly, then turned away and strode back to the dresser, where he'd left the other can. It issued a tiny hiss as he popped it open. He took a long swig of soda straight from the can.

Annie was relieved by his choice of beverage, but she didn't comment on it. She was even more relieved by Keith's having come back as quickly as he did. Despite his withdrawal from her, his decision to return to the room implied that he was willing to confront the agonizing issue that had sprung up between them, denying them the intimacy they'd come so close to sharing.

"I still miss him," she admitted, hoping to put Keith at ease by speaking first. "Do you?"

Keith almost looked at Annie—almost, but not quite. He nodded, then leaned his hips against the dresser and drank some more of his soda.

Annie ran her finger over the frosty glass, tracing a series of arching lines through the film of condensation. Then she turned back to Keith. His legs were extended in front of him, spread slightly apart, and she tried not to dwell on how long they were, and how strong, how hard his thighs were, how narrow his hips, how trim his waist. She steered her attention to his face, to the growth of hair darkening his jaw and to his eyes, which were darkened by memories. Sometimes, those smoky gray eyes had an incredibly erotic effect on Annie. But not tonight, not anymore. They forced her to think only of Adam, of loss.

"At first," she continued when Keith remained silent, "I missed Adam the way he was, as an infant. Now, mostly, when I miss him, I find myself missing what he might have become if he'd survived. I imagine him as a little boy, running around, playing ball. I picture him going to school and learning to read and write. Or all grown up, getting married and making me a grandmother."

Keith nodded again. He shifted his gaze from the closed curtains to Annie. This time he let his eyes meet hers bravely. They appeared infinitely dark and resolutely dry. He hadn't wept when Adam died; Annie didn't suppose he was going to weep now.

She wished he would say something, but he didn't. His penetrating stare seemed to draw her words out. "I felt unbelievably guilty, at first. I was sure it was my fault that he'd died. I kept eating myself up with the thought that if only I'd done something differently, if only I'd known he was high risk, or if I'd gotten out of bed earlier that morning, or..." She faltered, fighting off a wave of anguish.

"When I felt guilty," Keith commented, his tone low and rusty but enormously welcome to Annie's ears, "it was more a matter of feeling biologically at fault. I supplied the seed, after all. I kept thinking that maybe he died because my genes weren't good enough."

As grateful as she was for Keith's having finally spoken, she was equally shocked by what he'd said. She had experienced all manner of guilt after Adam had died, but never guilt over the condition of her genes. What shocked her most about Keith's statement, however, was that he'd admitted to something so personal, so private. He had never expressed such an emotion—or any emotions at all—at the time of Adam's death.

"You were right," Keith conceded, pushing himself away from the dresser and crossing over to the bed. He sat on it, not too close to Annie but closer than he'd been, and addressed his can of soda. "Stopping us, I mean. I've always...it's not as if I've been running around like a sex-crazed stud, but...I've been with a few women since we split. I was always a boy scout, Annie, always prepared, always careful. I don't know why I...with you..." He broke off, shaking his head. Then he took another sip of soda, swallowed and looked away.

Annie pondered his fragmented words. Of course Keith was a careful man, of course he was mature and responsible. Perhaps his rage, when Annie had brought things to a halt, had resulted from frustration with himself in having not been prepared this time.

Except that, as he'd admitted, he had come to Brenton without any expectation that he and Annie would rediscover their love. He hadn't planned to make love with her; why should he have been prepared for it?

If she dug deep enough, she believed she'd find a compliment imbedded in his words. The first time Keith had kissed her after his arrival in Connecticut, he'd been fully in control. Tonight, he hadn't been. He'd been more carried away than she was. She had been the one to cool things down; she'd been the one to inject some sanity into the situation.

Keith had been swept up by the impulse. Maybe it had nothing to do with love; maybe it had merely been a half-crazed longing to recapture the past, or to put an end to a string of lonely nights. Maybe his desire for Annie tonight was just as illogical as his desire to take over an established law practice and move to Brenton, just as illogical as his obsessive years-long search for Annie.

"Why did you find me?" she asked, for what she hoped was the final time. She was no longer exasperated by Keith's difficulty in answering. But she was desperate to know his answer.

He turned his head, tilting it, gazing at her from a funny angle. He offered her another smile, one so poignant it seemed to reach through her chest and squeeze her heart. "You think I came so I could talk to you about Adam," he mused.

"I don't know, Keith. Is that the reason?"

He exhaled. "I guess . . . I guess I came because I'm still trying to exorcise some ghosts," he allowed. He drained his can of soda, lofted it neatly into the garbage pail across the room, and stretched out on his side, balancing his elbow on the mattress and cradling his head in his hand. "Part of the guilt was biological, Annie, and part of it was paternal. I don't think . . ." He closed his eyes; Annie inferred that he was wrestling with one of his ghosts now. "I don't think I was a very good father."

"Of course you were," she said.

"I wasn't. I came and went, Annie. I was never really in the thick of it. I spent more time with Jose Alvaredo and his UFW cronies than I did with you and Adam."

"You were doing important work—"

"Bull. Adam was more important. I knew it even then, but . . ." He glanced away and cursed.

Annie longed to climb onto the bed beside Keith, to wrap her arms around him, to hug him and console him and reassure him that she couldn't have asked for a better father for her son. But she didn't dare. Even though Keith was confessing his darkest, most agonizing secrets to her, she still sensed a reservoir of anger within him—and she couldn't fight the suspicion that that anger was directed toward her as well as himself.

And in all honesty, she had to agree with his assessment of his performance as a father. He hadn't been in the thick of it. Adam had always been primarily Annie's responsibility.

Aware that her question was risky, she took a deep breath for fortitude before asking, "If you felt you weren't being a good father for Adam, why didn't you do something about it?"

"Because," Keith flared. His voice was low and taut, the anger bubbling to the surface but not quite boiling over. "Because you shut me out, Annie. You shut me out when he was alive, and you shut me out even more when he died."

"Shut you out?" she echoed, bewildered. "I would have loved it if you'd helped—"

"*Helped?*" He issued a derisive laugh. "*Helped?* As if you were the boss, and I was mother's little helper? He was *my* son, Annie. And you relegated me to the role of assistant parent. It took me two damned years to realize that I had as much right to miss Adam as you did. He was *mine*, too."

"Of course he was," she snapped, her fury matching Keith's. If he'd wanted to be more of a father to Adam, he'd had plenty of opportunity. But he hadn't bothered, he hadn't given of himself. He'd been working long hours, not only to earn money to support the family but because he'd elected to take the toughest legal cases. He could have put in less time and still earned enough to pay the bills. He could have taken a less demanding job. He'd made his choices. Annie hadn't relegated him to a secondary role—he'd chosen that role for himself. "All you had to do," she said grittily, "was take over. I would have gladly let you change the diapers, take Adam on walks, give him his baths, do the night feedings—"

"I couldn't have done the night feedings," Keith pointed out, his voice suddenly devoid of anger. He sounded weary, unwilling to rise to the battle. "You were nursing him, Annie. Don't you see? You were nursing him from your own body. It was something I couldn't do, just as I couldn't carry him inside me. You nursed him, you raised him—you were on his wavelength. You and he were a closed society. I couldn't—" He cleared the catch in his throat. "I couldn't find my way inside, Annie. And then, when he died..." He drifted off again.

"When he died...?" Annie gently prodded him, also willing to let the fight end.

Keith rolled onto his back and stared at the ceiling, his expression full of hurt. "You closed me out even more. You didn't turn to me for comfort. You turned to your damned support group in Chico."

Annie's mouth fell open. Once more, she felt shocked—shell-shocked. Keith was dropping his explosive revelations on her, and she couldn't absorb the bombardment.

But one thing she was positive about was that she wouldn't have had to rely on the support group for parents of SIDS victims if she'd gotten the comfort she had needed from Keith. "You didn't understand," she charged, leaning forward and forcing out the words. "You didn't even try to understand my pain. You didn't want to talk about it. You thought all you had to do was get rid of the baby furniture, and everything would be all better. They understood, Keith, and you refused to. That's why I turned to them."

"You refused to understand me, too," Keith retorted bitterly. "Do you want to know why I left? Because you refused to understand me. If you ask me, Annie, you left first. You may have stayed in the house in Orland, but you left me long before I left you. All I did was to make it real."

Stunned by his harsh accusation, she stood and marched to the window. She pushed the curtains back and struggled to crank open the window. After some resistance, the crank began to turn, and the windowpane angled out. Annie drank in the cool night air, praying for it to clear her mind.

She couldn't believe what Keith was saying. She leave him? He was the one who'd packed his things and departed. He was the one who'd sat her down on the living-room sofa one hot July evening, handed her a bottle of beer, and said, "Look, Annie. I need a breather. I love you, but I just can't stay here anymore. I know you're okay, I know you'll be able to handle things if I go. But right now, I need some time to myself."

She heard his voice shaping the words. She pictured him as he'd looked then: his hair a solid dark color, without a trace of gray, his dimples more prominent, his laugh lines barely visible at the outer corners of his eyes. He had been wearing jeans that night, just like tonight, and a white oxford shirt much like the shirt he was wearing now. He'd spoken in a soft, level voice, calmly outlining a more than fair division of their meager assets, explaining how he planned to transfer the lease into her name if she wished to remain in the house, offering to send her his own version of alimony until she got a job.

She had tried to match his poise, but inside she'd been dying. She loved him more than she'd thought it possible to love a man, and he was leaving her.

"I loved you," she murmured, turning away from the window. She said it without rage or resentment, and the corners of her lips turned upward in a small, rueful smile. "I loved you, Keith, and you broke my heart. That's how I remember it."

While Annie had had her back to him, Keith had raised himself to sit again. His hair was tousled, his clothing creased. But his eyes burned into her, making her regret that she'd revealed her soul to him. She hadn't mentioned anything about love six years ago, when he'd been working out the mechanics of his departure. She hadn't told him then that he was breaking her heart; she'd had too much pride.

She ought to have held onto her pride this time, too. But it was too late. She couldn't retract her words.

Sighing, she let the curtain fall back into place, strode across the room to fetch her purse, and then headed for the door. "I'm going now, Keith," she said.

He stood, but he didn't approach. Nor did he say anything—not a plea for her to stay, not a farewell. Nothing. All she felt from him was his gaze, still burning, burning through her as she turned the knob, pushed the door open, and left the room.

There were a lot of possibilities: pummeling the walls, kicking the furniture, breaking whatever was breakable and handy. Screaming. Chasing her, catching her before she reached her car, dragging her back to the room and hurling himself at her feet, begging her to forgive him.

Instead, Keith lifted her half-consumed can of soda from the pedestal table, carried it into the bathroom and poured the effervescent brown fluid down the drain. Then he flattened the can—a bit of punching and hitting was involved, but nothing particularly cathartic—and tossed it into the wastebasket.

He wouldn't chase Annie. He wouldn't drag her anywhere. Most of all, he wouldn't apologize to her. What he'd said had been the truth.

What amazed Keith was that he hadn't been wholly aware of the truth until just now, when he'd voiced it. He had harbored an undefined resentment toward Annie when Adam was born, and he'd assumed that it was the stereotypical male reaction to being displaced as the sole focus of his woman's life. Lots of husbands reacted to their newborn children that way.

Keith hadn't doubted that Annie loved him—but Adam was the center of her universe. At the time, Keith had conceded that this was the way it was supposed to be, the way it should be. But he felt left out. And then, when Adam died, he felt even more left out.

"Talk about guilt," he muttered aloud as the memory blossomed fully in his mind. He'd been furious with Annie for shutting him out in her grief. Resentment was too mild a word for what he'd felt. And when he wasn't seething with anger, he'd been tortured with guilt: how dare he criticize Annie's way of mourning? What kind of a self-centered jerk must he be to condemn Annie for her particular style of sorrow?

The only way he could deal with it had been to deny that he felt anything at all. For months afterward, whenever the feelings began to creep up on him, he left town, or numbed himself with booze. Eventually, he realized that he was allowed to feel bad about Adam's death. But not until tonight, when he recognized how much he still loved Annie, had he also allowed himself to admit how much he still resented her.

He did love her. No matter that they'd just exchanged some pretty hostile words, no matter that she'd just accused him of breaking her heart and then stormed out on him—he loved her.

He dived back onto the bed and buried his head in one of the pillows, which held the faint scent of her. He was entitled to be angry; his bitterness toward Annie was legitimate. But all he could think about was the velvety softness of her skin and the slippery texture of her hair as it spilled through his fingers, the sweetness of her mouth and the rising and falling of her body beneath his.

Nothing in his life had ever felt as good as Annie, then or now. He hoped that, in time, he would be able to feel something that good again, when both he and Annie were ready for it. She wasn't ready yet, and—though it astonished him to admit it—neither was he.

Somewhere around two o'clock in the morning, Annie woke to the distant rumble of an airplane flying over her house. It was a muffled roar, too quiet to have awakened her if she'd been deeply asleep. Or perhaps there was no airplane at all; perhaps she'd simply dreamed the sound.

Real or not, the airplane reminded Annie of Keith. She squinted at the red digits on her alarm clock and groaned. In less than ten hours, Keith would be on an airplane, flying away.

Why was it that they were always fated to run from each other? Why couldn't they complete anything, whether a conversation or an act of love? Annie was certain she'd been right to stop both—the act of love and the ensuing argument—but now, in the thick darkness of night, she simmered with doubt, questions, a yearning to be with Keith, to talk if not to love him.

What bothered her most was the possibility that Keith might be right. Maybe she *had* closed him out.

Memories were tricky; people tended to remember what they wanted to, or what they could cope with, and discarded the rest. In Annie's memories, she hadn't deliberately closed Keith out of anything. From the moment of conception on, she'd wanted him fully involved in their baby's existence. And certainly after Adam's death, she'd wanted Keith to be with her.

But he couldn't have invented his feelings. If he remembered that Annie had closed him out, did it really matter that she remembered differently?

She'd never meant to hurt him, though. He'd never meant to hurt her, either. What a mess they'd made of it.

And now he was leaving, before they'd have a chance to set things right again. Before she could find out what she'd done to hurt him or what she could do to make it better, he would be gone, leaving her with her own brand-new army of ghosts to exorcise.

If she fell back to sleep at all, it was a shallow rest, a drifting in and out of consciousness. By the time the alarm clock buzzed to awaken her, she was already out of bed, opening the curtains. The sky outside her window hung low with thick, slate-gray clouds. She wondered whether Keith's plane would be able to take off on such an overcast day.

Of course it would; weather rarely prevented jets from flying. She couldn't count on a few clouds to keep Keith in Connecticut.

She had a busy day at the library. The head librarian had written up a budget proposal for the next fiscal year, and Annie had to analyze the expenditures and calculate whether the children's library could survive within the budget. A box containing two dozen children's records, which had been given up for lost, was discovered by a janitor in the basement of the elementary school, and Annie had to inspect and recatalog all the records. Early in the afternoon, a frenetic mother came in, demanding a list of all the children's videotapes available for viewing. Her son's birthday party was scheduled for that Saturday, she explained, and all the children were showing videos at their birthday parties these days.

Once she had helped the woman select a few appropriate cartoons for her son's party, Annie found herself facing a lull. She glanced up at the clock above the door: two-fifteen. Keith was somewhere over the Rockies, she estimated, thousands of feet above the earth, flying west, widening the distance between her and himself.

Not two weeks ago—not one day ago—all Annie had wanted was for him to leave. Now, she was tormented by his departure when so much remained unresolved between them.

"Hey, Annie!"

Annie wrestled with a reflexive grimace. The last person she wanted to see right now was Justine Willis. But she presented the girl with a faint smile and said, "Hello, Justine."

Justine bounced down the stairs, swinging her schoolbag wildly. "My mom has to run some errands today," Justine reported, tossing the bag onto the counter and unsnapping her raincoat. "She said I should come straight here—"

"I'm sure she did," Annie confirmed dryly. She had heard Justine's speech many times before.

"How's Mr. Chips?" Justine asked, removing her raincoat and jogging over to the bird cage. "I've got some cookies in my schoolbag. Is it all right if I give him one?"

"I don't think he can handle sweets," Annie said. Justine had been calling the parakeet "Mr. Chips" ever since Keith had suggested the name, but today...today, hearing the name bothered Annie. Today, she supposed, anything that reminded her of Keith would bother her.

Justine's reference to the bird as "Mr. Chips" reminded Annie not just of Keith but of the afternoon he'd visited her in the library. He'd been so kind to Justine that day, so friendly. Annie had been astounded by his friendliness toward the little girl.

Why hadn't she recognized his sensitivity six years ago, or seven, or eight? Why hadn't she realized that Keith had a generous heart and a warm soul, that he loved children at least as much as Annie did?

Chastising herself for her past blindness wasn't going to do any good. But being patient with Justine might. Annie had a lot to learn from Keith, and she was willing to start with this. "Here, Justine," she said, pulling the box of birdseed from the shelf where she kept it and carrying it to the cage. "If you'd really like to feed Mr. Chips, let me get you his dish, and you can fill it up." The bird chirped gleefully as Annie slid out his empty dish. She realized that this was the first time she'd actually called him "Mr. Chips."

Justine greeted her task with enthusiasm—so much enthusiasm that a small mountain of birdseed wound up on the floor. Annie smothered the temptation to scold, and instead armed Justine with a dustpan and broom. Together they cleaned up the mess.

"I guess you want me to do my homework, huh," Justine remarked once they'd finished at the bird cage.

Annie eyed the child with surprise. Justine had never volunteered to do her homework before. Annie had always had to tell her to do it.

All she needed was a little attention, Annie realized. All Justine wanted was someone to talk to, someone to keep her company and indulge her for a few minutes, and then she'd pipe down and leave Annie alone. Annie smiled as Justine lifted her schoolbag and carried it to the table near the play corner. Without another word, Justine unlatched the bag, pulled out a workbook and pencil, and began her homework.

Annie settled down at the computer and clicked it on, planning to review the annual budget one more time. But her gaze drifted to Justine. Annie saw not the dark-haired, dark-eyed girl but her own child, an imaginary Adam at the age of seven, with flaxen hair like his mother and dark gray eyes like his father. She imagined him doing his homework not at the table in the Brenton Town Library but at the kitchen table in the house in Orland. Annie imagined him swinging his feet back and forth as he worked, chewing on his eraser, eyeing the clock. It would read six o'clock, then seven, then seven-thirty... and then Keith would come through the kitchen door after another long day in his storefront office. Adam would fling down his pencil, leap from his chair and jump into Keith's arms, shouting, "Daddy! Daddy!" And Keith would hug him, swing him around, shower his face with kisses....

Keith had been a good father. A damned good father. And if he didn't know it by now, Annie would have to prove it to him, if only so he could get on with his life.

She had to see him. She had to get him to come back. They had to finish what they'd begun, or the past would never let go of them.

Seven

As usual, Wilshire Boulevard was congested with traffic. Keith gazed down through the sealed window of his office and watched a particularly daring sports car as it weaved recklessly from lane to lane. At one point it strayed across the centerline in an attempt to pass a slower-moving car.

A month ago, Keith's reaction to such a scene might have been: "There's a potential lawsuit somewhere in there." Today, his only reaction was: "I wish I were in Brenton, where lawyers ride bicycles and windows open up."

The central air-conditioning was functioning, ventilating the offices in the skyscraper and maintaining the interior at a pleasantly mild temperature. But Keith would have preferred to be breathing the outdoor air, even if it was stagnant and smoggy. He had removed his jacket as soon as he'd entered the office after lunch, and his tie hung loose from his unbuttoned collar. He supposed he'd have to wear neckties when he took clients out to lunch in Connecticut, too—and he'd have to transport his clients to restaurants in a car, not on the handlebars of a bicycle. But somehow it was easy to idealize Brenton. It was easy, especially at a distance of three thousand miles, to imagine that everything was perfect there, that Keith's work would always be meaningful, that the New England breezes would always be balmy, neither too hot nor too cold, and that he would never again have to contend with anything like the abominable freeway traffic of the greater Los Angeles area.

His car. Should he sell it and buy a new car in Connecticut, or should he drive his trusty Subaru across the country?

The particulars of closing down his life in Los Angeles were tedious, but Keith was handling them with reasonable efficiency. He'd already engaged in several frank discussions with the firm's partners, explaining his desire to leave. They'd accepted his decision without putting up too much of a fuss, although they seemed bemused by it. It was inconceivable to them that anyone—especially someone with Keith's skills and ability—would voluntarily abandon the fast track for an underpaid practice in the hinterlands. "It snows in Connecticut," one of the partners had pointed out. "Not ski snow, Keith, but close-the-roads snow! Is that really what you want?"

Keith had assured his superiors that, close-the-roads snow notwithstanding, a private legal practice in Brenton was exactly what he wanted. The partners had negotiated the financial aspects of terminating Keith's association with the firm, and they'd magnanimously offered him free access to his office for as long as he needed it.

The client that Keith had taken to lunch today was someone whose case had just reached a settlement. When he'd flown to Connecticut a couple of weeks ago, he'd had one other case pending, and that client had agreed to let one of Keith's colleagues at the firm take it over for him. Keith still had reams of paperwork to complete before he'd be able to leave the firm, and he'd committed himself to assisting an associate on an upcoming class-action suit. But slowly, he was tying up loose ends and bringing this season of his life to a tidy close.

The telephone on his desk buzzed, and he abandoned the window and strode across the tiny room to answer it. Ironically, although he had little actual work left, his desk was much more cluttered than it used to be when he was up to his ears in cases. He had to exhume his telephone from beneath a yellow legal pad and a mountain of wrinkled notepapers before he could answer it. "Yes?"

"Keith," said Betty, the secretary he shared with two other associates, "there's a call for you from a woman named Annie Jameson."

Annie. Keith closed his eyes and sank onto his chair. Annie. Annie was on the line.

He'd been busy since his arrival in California—busy finalizing his cases, justifying his plans to his friends, advertising for potential tenants to sublet his apartment. He'd been busy checking out the fees of various moving companies. He'd been busy swimming laps every single day, swimming until his arms and legs were limp and his lungs ached.

He'd been keeping himself busy so that he wouldn't have to think, so that he wouldn't have to face certain issues. After six years, he ought to have adopted newer, more effective tactics, but he hadn't. He still relied on keeping busy to avoid confronting his confusion, his guilt, his fear.

A week had elapsed since Annie walked out of his motel room. A week since he'd last seen her, last spoken to her. Every evening when he'd arrived home from the office, he'd started to dial her number—and then, unsure about what he ought to say, he'd decided he had to "clear his head" or "sort his thoughts," and the means he'd chosen to attain mental clarity was a mile-long swim in the apartment complex pool. By the time he'd returned to his apartment, showered and dressed, it had been seven-thirty or eight o'clock, too late to phone someone three times zones to the east.

All those miles of swimming were doing wonders for Keith's physique, but nothing for his head. Certain things he knew: he loved Annie; thinking about her body, her hair, her dazzling blue eyes and her irresistible lips made him want her beyond belief; he admired what she'd accomplished in her life; he was sorry he'd hurt her six years ago.

He knew, as well, that she'd managed to hurt him rather spectacularly six years ago and that, far from being sorry, she didn't even seem willing to acknowledge that she'd done anything wrong.

He wanted to go back to her, and he would. But before he could, he had to heal. He hadn't even realized how much healing he still had to do—how much anger he had to over-come—until he'd seen her.

He probably should have phoned her, though, despite his ambivalence. It would have spared him this unanticipated call. How had she reached him, anyway? He'd never given her his number or the name of his firm. He would have, if she'd asked for it, but she hadn't asked.

All of which was irrelevant, he admitted. However she'd found him, she was now on the line. Without a clue of what to expect or how to react, he thanked Betty, pressed the flashing button on his phone console and said, "Hello, Annie."

Tracking Keith down had been the simple part. Knowing what to say to him, now that she'd succeeded, was some-thing else.

As difficult as it had been for Keith to find her, Annie imagined that even a three-year-long search incorporating white lies and bribes couldn't have been as difficult as coming up with the right opening line once he'd found her. But he'd had those three years to prepare for their meeting, and he'd had no preconceived notions about what Annie would be like if he did find her. It had to be easier to talk to a stranger than to talk to someone you loved and longed for—and didn't understand.

At first, she had assumed that Keith would contact her. Their parting had been less than amicable, but still, it made sense to Annie that if anyone called anyone, Keith would be the one to do the calling. He knew where she was; he knew her address, her phone number, her place of business. Annie didn't even know what city he lived in.

Besides, he was the aggressor in all this. He was the one who'd left her in Orland, who'd hunted her, who'd found her. He was the actor, the doer.

But what did that make her? The passive one? The acted-upon one? Annie had too much gumption to sit around doing nothing while she waited for Keith to touch base with her—especially when she desperately yearned to talk to him. Now that they'd had their fight and the dust had cleared, she needed to know whether Keith still intended to move to Brenton, and whether he still loved her. She needed to see him again, even though she wasn't sure what she would do if she did see him. It was the same kind of need he'd felt when he'd come to see her—a blind obsession.

When he hadn't called her by the weekend, she began her search for him. She phoned Directory Assistance for the city of Los Angeles, and when the operator couldn't find a listing for Keith LaMotte, Annie tried Long Beach, Anaheim, Santa Monica and Woodland Hills. She considered calling Newport Beach, where Keith's parents lived—or at least where they had lived six years ago—but she didn't have the nerve. His parents were as likely to hang up on her as hers had been to hang up on him.

Instead, she called her sister. "Annie!" Teri greeted her exuberantly, shouting above the whine of an electric motor. "I can't talk now—I'm busy fixing a gourmet dinner for the folks. I'm going to introduce them to Craig tonight, and I want them stuffed for the occasion. I'm making—are you ready for this?—salmon mousse. You wouldn't believe how complicated this recipe is, Annie..."

"I'll only take a minute," Annie promised. "I just want to ask you one question: When Keith visited you, did he happen to mention where he was living?"

"Huh? Wait, hang on a minute." The motor noise ceased and Teri came back on the line. "I had to turn off the food processor. Now—what did you say?"

"Did Keith ever tell you what town he was living in?"

Teri cursed softly. "You really said what I thought you said. I can't blame it on the food processor." She sighed. "All right, what's going on? Did he fly the coop?"

"Yes."

"And the creep didn't leave a forwarding address?"

Annie grimaced. Teri's phrasing was uncomfortably blunt but accurate. "That's right," she granted.

"So why the hell do you want to track him down?"

"Because," Annie answered, then realized she owed her sister more of an explanation than that. "Because we've got unfinished business."

"You two are going to have unfinished business for the rest of your lives," Teri pointed out grimly. "Get used to it, Annie. It's time to move on. Don't give him a chance to do another number on you."

Annie groaned. Teri was preoccupied with her elegant dinner preparations; now wasn't a good time for Annie to explain that, however unintentionally, she had done a number on Keith, too. "I'm not asking for advice, Teri," she pointed out. "I'm just trying to find out where he lives. Please—do you remember? Did he tell you?"

Teri relented with a disgruntled sigh. "Altadena, maybe? Something like that. I don't really remember."

"Thanks," Annie said, hoping her elation wasn't evident to her sister. "Thanks so much, Teri. Have fun tonight. I hope it all goes well."

"Keep me posted," Teri requested. "If you wind up in a million pieces again, Annie, come to Portland and I'll put you back together. I've got the bed in the spare bedroom all made up for you."

Not bothering to remark on Teri's pessimism, not wishing to consider the possibility that she might once again wind up in a million pieces, Annie thanked her sister one more time and bade her goodbye. Then she called up Altadena's Directory Assistance. No Keith LaMotte.

She stewed over it for a couple of days. If Keith could locate her through the American Library Association, perhaps she could locate him through the American Bar Association. Or, if he didn't contact her within a week or so, she could muster enough courage to telephone his parents.

Or she could talk to Beatrice McKenna.

Beatrice arrived to pick up her granddaughter after Annie's weekly story hour for preschoolers. The group had been noisier than usual; several children had begged Annie to read *Cinderella* again, and then, much to her surprise, one of the children hollered that he wanted to hear "Sophie the Dragon." "You told that story at Shandler's," the boy reminded her. "It was great."

"But it's not from a book," Annie objected. "I made it up."

"So what? Tell it again!"

"Tell *Cinderella* again!" shouted Steve Harper's daughter, Jennifer.

"I was going to read *The Story of Ferdinand* and *Where the Wild Things Are* this week," Annie informed the group.

"But if you all behave yourselves, maybe we'll have time for *Cinderella*, too."

As it turned out, not only did she have time for the books she'd planned and *Cinderella*, but also for an abbreviated version of "Sophie the Dragon." The enthusiastic reception her own story received was ego gratifying, and she was feeling extremely proud of her creativity by the time the parents started arriving to pick up their children. Wheeling her chair from the play corner back to the counter, she spotted Beatrice McKenna descending the steps.

Annie knew Beatrice only casually. Although Beatrice always dressed youthfully and wore her silver hair in a short, chic style, Annie felt deferential toward her. Beatrice and her husband were pillars of the Brenton community.

Still, Annie wasn't about to let this opportunity pass. "Mrs. McKenna?" she called to Beatrice.

Beatrice turned toward the counter and smiled. "Hello, Annie," she returned the greeting. "I'm here to get Erica. Was she well behaved today?"

"Yes, Mrs. McKenna." A twinge of nervousness prompted Annie to fidget with her dater and stamp pad. "Could I please speak with you for a minute before you get Erica?"

Beatrice glanced toward the play corner, where her granddaughter and two other children were engrossed in a make-believe tea party with a few doll-size dishes. Satisfied, Beatrice approached the counter and unbuttoned her suede jacket. "Is anything wrong?" she asked, gazing curiously at Annie.

"No. I'm—" She smiled edgily, then drew in a breath and proceeded. "I understand your husband is planning to retire."

Beatrice registered surprise. Then her face relaxed into its usual handsome smile. "If you need some legal assistance, Annie, just give him a call. If I had anything to say in the matter, he would have retired years ago, but, stubborn mule that he is, he's dragging it out. He swears he's going to cut down on his work load, but if your problem is nothing too complicated—"

"No, I don't need a lawyer," Annie assured Beatrice, silently chastising herself for beating around the bush. Taking another deep breath, she plunged in: "Actually, I'm wondering whether he's worked everything out with Keith LaMotte."

"Keith LaMotte?" Beatrice's gray eyebrows arched, and her smile increased. "Do you know him?"

"Yes, I do."

"My goodness, he made friends quickly in town," Beatrice remarked. "I suppose it's not that startling, though. He's such a charming young man."

"I didn't just meet him," Annie hastened to explain. "We—we go way back. We were friends in college."

"You were? What a coincidence!" Beatrice exclaimed. "I wonder why he didn't say anything about it to George. Brenton is such a small town. Keith should have mentioned it."

Annie experienced a sense of deflation. When Keith had found her at Shandler's Department Store, he'd identified himself to Tim Shandler as Annie's ex-husband. With the McKennas, he hadn't bothered to tell them he knew her.

She considered getting even with him by telling Beatrice that she was Keith's ex-wife. As Keith himself had admitted, it wouldn't be that far from the truth. Annie had worn his ring, given birth to his child—

"If you wouldn't be divulging any secrets," she said quickly, refusing to linger on thoughts of Adam, "I was wondering how the talks between Keith and your husband are going.''

"Oh, they're already settled,'' Beatrice said excitedly. "As I understand it, all that's pending is Keith's move east. Given the work he has to finish at his law firm in Los Angeles, I suppose that's going to take some time. But then, I'm used to waiting for George to retire. What's another few months?''

A few months? Was it going to take Keith a few months to come back to Connecticut? Maybe Beatrice was willing to wait that long for her husband, but Annie would go crazy if she had to wait that long for Keith to return. "You wouldn't by any chance know the name of the law firm he's with in Los Angeles, would you?'' she asked, hoping she sounded nonchalant.

"Oh, heavens, what was the name?'' Beatrice frowned as she tried to remember. "You know those firms—six last names tacked together with a lot of commas. Hello, Erica,'' she crooned as her granddaughter raced up to her and hugged her legs. "George must know,'' Beatrice said, turning back to Annie. "But for the life of me—''

Annie was sure she'd exhausted her supply of bravery talking to Beatrice. She doubted she'd be able to summon the courage necessary to talk to George. "Do you remember anything about the firm?'' she asked, doing her best to disguise her eagerness. "Any of the names? The address?'' Noticing Beatrice's mildly suspicious look, Annie added, "I'd like to surprise him at work with something—you know, one of those singing messengers. A gag. To welcome him to Brenton in advance.'' Much as she hated lying, she was pleased with the fib she'd concocted. It sounded plausible.

Beatrice grinned. "Wilshire Boulevard,'' she confided. "I do remember that. And I think...oh, lord, what were those names? Samuels, that was one. Samuels or Michaels. Dillinger—that was another. I remember them making jokes about John Dillinger.''

"Thank you," Annie said effusively. "Thanks so much."

"My pleasure." Beatrice leaned conspiratorially toward Annie. "I won't breathe a hint of this conversation to George. I don't want him to spoil your surprise by leaking word of it to Keith. And listen—why just a singing telegram? Why don't you send him one of those men in the gorilla suits? Or a belly dancer, maybe."

"I'll think about it," Annie mumbled, trying not to look too startled. The woman had depths to her that Annie had never suspected before. Erica, Annie concluded, was lucky to have a grandmother as lively as Beatrice McKenna.

Annie grew restless waiting for her lunchtime replacement—one of the assistant librarians from the adult section upstairs—to arrive. As soon as the woman did, Annie dashed up the stairs and headed for the Reference Room. The library didn't possess every telephone book published in the country, but they had directories for the big cities. With a friendly nod toward the reference librarian, Annie hurried to the collection of phone books and tugged the thick Los Angeles directory from the shelf.

She flipped to the yellow pages and ran her index finger down row after row of attorneys, praying for the right combination of names to leap out at her. Midway through the second page, it did: "Michaels, Bavarro, Dillinger, Stein & Samson," with a Wilshire Boulevard address. Annie scribbled the number on a sheet of note paper, folded it twice, and tucked it into her shirt pocket, next to her heart. She was so elated by her find that she temporarily forgot to worry about what she'd say to Keith when she reached him, or how she'd survive whatever he might have to say to her.

Her elation carried her through the afternoon. When work didn't require her full concentration, she allowed her mind to drift. She thought about the Cinderella story—not the archetypical myth about the poor but virtuous toiler being transformed into a princess, but the other part of the tale, about the prince who so wants to find Cinderella that he searches the entire kingdom with a glass slipper in his hand. Keith had searched for her with that same single-mindedness, and this week, she had searched for him. Whatever their problems, she couldn't shake the notion that he was the only man who fit. How else to explain why she'd fallen in love with him? Only one man fit the imaginary shoe; only one man fit her love.

She thought about Cinderella and the prince, and she thought about Sophie the dragon, who blew magical multicolored smoke through her nostrils. Keith might be the only man who fit, but there was still a lot of fear to overcome. If they could see their way through the smoke to the rainbow, Annie was certain they would be all right. But if they couldn't . . .

Her apprehension increased as the hands of the clock approached closing time, as she locked up the children's library and drove home. With a determination made of false courage, she marched into her bedroom, lifted her telephone from the night table and started to dial the number she'd written down in the library.

Halfway through the number, she hesitated. What should she say to him? How was she supposed to ignore her fear? What if he wasn't able to ignore his?

Acknowledging her fear was half the battle, and the courage that infused her didn't seem so artificial, after all. This was *Keith*, she reflected. She had nothing to be afraid of.

The last time she'd taken that attitude, of course, she had nearly made love to Keith in his motel room. And she had ended up storming away from him in pain and anger. Just when that memory dawned on her, a secretary answered the phone and recited the law firm's name. Almost hoping the secretary wouldn't know whom Annie was talking about, she asked for Keith LaMotte.

Bull's-eye. "One moment please—I'll see if he's in," said the secretary before putting Annie on hold.

Maybe he wasn't in. Maybe he was in but didn't want to speak to Annie, and he'd tell the secretary to cover for him. Maybe— "Hello, Annie," he said.

"Hello, Keith." Now what? Should she be courteous and ask how he was? Should she be forthright and demand an explanation for his failure to call her? Before she could make up her mind, her mouth betrayed her by letting the truth slip out: "I miss you."

Oh, lord. Why on earth had she said that? After berating herself for revealing her most profound emotions to Keith in the motel room a week ago, here she was again, revealing herself, exposing her vulnerability. She was so mortified, she nearly didn't hear him say, "I miss you, too."

"You do? You've got a funny way of showing it."

"In other words, why didn't I call you?" Keith summarized. He lapsed into a lengthy silence, then said, "Would it be enough to say it's been hectic here?"

"No," Annie countered in a gentle but firm voice. "That wouldn't be enough. True Confessions, Keith. Why haven't you called me?"

He sighed. "We shouldn't be discussing this on the phone."

"We haven't got much choice," she observed. "Are you angry with me?"

He sighed again. "You know the answer to that, Annie."

All right. He was angry; she was angry with him, too. And while she agreed with Keith that they shouldn't discuss this on the phone, she didn't see any alternative. "I've been going over and over what you said, Keith. If I hurt you...it was accidental. I never even realized—you never let on—"

"Annie," Keith silenced her. "We can't talk about this now, okay?"

"When can we?" It was as good a way as any to find out when Keith would be coming to Connecticut.

"Oh, Annie, I don't know. I promised one of my colleagues here that I'd assist on a complicated case he's taken on. They've set a court date for two weeks from now, but there might be a postponement. And I've got so much other stuff to take care of—"

"Look," she cut him off, growing impatient. "If it's too much effort, Keith, skip it. As Teri said, we'll always have unfinished business between us. So why don't we just give up, and you can stay in California. Not every story gets to have a neat ending."

"No, Annie," Keith argued, his tone low and hoarse. "I'm not going to stay in California. I want you. That part hasn't changed." He exhaled, and when he spoke again, he sounded equally impatient. "Do you really think I haven't called you because I didn't feel like it? Do you think I've conveniently forgotten about you? Annie, every day, every single day since I've been here, I've started to call you. More than once I've made it all the way to the last digit before I hung up."

"Why?" Annie asked, dumbfounded.

"Because I still haven't forgiven you," he confessed, his tone lower, thick with emotion. "Because I'm still mad at you. But I want you. It's like I'm schizoid, Annie—my brain keeps saying one thing, and my body something else. I want you so much... It's been such a long time since I've wanted a woman like this—but that's how I feel about you. Sometimes, I want you so much I don't even care what my brain is telling me." He cursed softly, then chuckled. "This is embarrassing, Annie," he whispered into the phone. "Here I am, sitting in my office, all turned on. Turn me off, would you? Say something disgusting."

"I want you, too," Annie admitted. It wasn't disgusting, and it wasn't going to turn him off. But it was an undeniable fact. Keith was being fiercely honest with her, and she had to reciprocate. "Keith, maybe..." She paused, groping through her snarled thoughts, trying to find a rational way of coping with the irrationalities of emotion. "Maybe we could just put our anger aside for a while. We could put it on hold until we were ready to deal with it."

He laughed again, a soft, helpless laugh. "You're incorrigible, Annie," he scolded. "You were like this back then, too. Whenever I tried to have a serious conversation with you, you'd start unbuttoning your blouse."

"I did not!"

"Remember the time I tried to explain the correlation between T-bills and the money market?"

Annie remembered well. In response to her innocent question, Keith had embarked on a pompous, long-winded lecture on how the dollar supply affected interest rates. He hadn't noticed her glazed expression or her deliberate yawning, so she'd resorted to the more effective strategy of seducing him. "I didn't unbutton my blouse," she disputed him. "I unbuttoned your jeans." It had worked, too. He had quickly discovered that there were more exciting things in life than predicting the future course of the nation's interest rates.

That Keith remembered, too, touched her. Confronting their mutual anger over Adam was much more important than analyzing money market rates, but Annie's and Keith's relationship didn't begin and end with Adam.

"This isn't working," Keith muttered huskily. "I'm still turned on."

"Then do something about it," Annie responded, half a plea and half a challenge. "Come back, Keith. Come back and see me. We should have finished at least this piece of business last week. We can finish the rest some other time."

"Annie." He was clearly tempted. "I have so much to do here, still . . ."

"I would come to you, Keith," Annie said, determined to maintain this level of honesty, "but I can't afford it. Small-town librarians earn zilch, and I'm still paying off the loans I had to take to pay for graduate school. You're in much better shape financially than I am, Keith. I know a round-trip ticket is expensive, but . . ." *But worth it,* she concluded silently.

"A weekend," he said, half to himself. Another bewildered laugh escaped him. "This is insane, Annie."

"It's the sanest thing we've done in six years."

"All right," he yielded. "Okay, Annie. One weekend. I can't spare any longer—"

"A weekend is fine," she assured him, wondering if he could hear the clamor of her heartbeat through the long-distance wire. It was practically deafening to her, a loud, rapid thrumming in her temples.

"Maybe I could fly out late Friday. I don't know, Annie. I'll have to work it out. I'll call you back tonight, okay?"

Annie didn't bother to remind him that it was already tonight in Connecticut. She didn't want to give him a chance to rethink anything. "Call me," she said, "as soon as you can."

Once she hung up, she realized that he would have plenty of time to rethink things before calling her back. Perhaps, once he'd cooled off, he would decide that listening to his brain made more sense than listening to his body. Perhaps he'd decide that, as much as he desired Annie, he resented her more. Perhaps he'd decide that flying east for a weekend was an extravagance he couldn't afford.

Sitting still gave her too much opportunity to think of all the reasons Keith could find for deciding not to come. She distracted herself by changing into a comfortable pair of jeans and heading for the kitchen, where she busied herself fixing a sandwich which she couldn't eat. After throwing it away, she wandered into the living room and flipped aimlessly through a magazine, her attention on the nerve-wracking silence of her house.

That silence was finally shattered by the ringing of the telephone. "I'm flying out of L.A.X. Friday night," Keith reported, his tone enigmatic. "It's an overnight flight. I'll be arriving in Hartford around nine o'clock Saturday morning. I'm going to be exhausted, Annie."

"I'll be there," Annie vowed. "Whatever condition you're in, I'll be there."

Eight

Annie arrived at the airport early; Keith arrived late. In the forty-five minute interval, she did her damnedest not to think. She knew that if she allowed a thought to enter her brain, it would probably concern the utter absurdity of what she and Keith were doing.

She didn't want to think, though. She wanted only to indulge in the romance of Keith's visit, the irresponsibility and extravagance of it. She wanted to luxuriate in the realization that he desired her enough to go this extraordinary length for her. She wanted to forget that a vital misunderstanding stood between them, threatening the happily-ever-after ending she longed for.

She would not allow the voice of reason to intrude. This weekend was a fantasy, and Annie wanted to hurl herself into it without doubts or qualms.

Keith looked tired when, at long last, his plane taxied to a halt at the terminal and discharged its passengers. His gait was slower than usual, his shoulders hunched beneath his denim jacket, and his eyelids drooped slightly. But his smile was warm when he glimpsed Annie in the waiting area, and he quickened his pace.

When he reached her, he threw his overnight bag onto the nearest chair and wrapped his arms around her. In that moment she understood that he was just as willing as she was to ignore reality for this weekend, to forget about their disagreements and resentments and pretend that the only thing that existed between them was their love.

He touched his lips lightly to hers. Gazing up into his face, she saw that beneath his drowsy lids his eyes were radiant, the color of flint at the moment a match sparks against it. "This sure beats the last time I flew in here," he admitted in a near whisper. "Tramping through the building alone, looking for the car rental desks. It's a lot nicer being met."

"Being met?" she teased, finding his phrasing rather impersonal. "I don't suppose it matters who's meeting you."

"You know it does," Keith murmured before kissing her again. "Let's go."

He released her and lifted his overnight bag, a soft-sided grip of brown leather. Although it was large, Annie was inexplicably disappointed when Keith told her he had no other luggage. She knew he would be leaving the following afternoon, but the fact that he'd traveled with only one piece of carry-on luggage stood as undeniable proof that he wasn't planning to stay.

Her disappointment directed itself inward. She mustn't expect any more of this weekend than what it was: one weekend. A brief hiatus in the ongoing struggle. Two carefree days. Nothing more.

They left the terminal and crossed a series of roadways to reach the short-term lot where Annie had left her car. Keith tossed his bag into the back seat, then folded himself onto the passenger seat beside Annie. She pulled out and navigated through the lot.

Neither of them spoke until they reached the highway. Trying to gauge his mood, Annie permitted herself an occasional glimpse of him. He was wearing jeans, she noticed, and a shirt and sweater under his jacket. His hair was slightly disheveled and his eyelids drooped lower, protecting his sleepy eyes from the slanting morning sunlight.

"It isn't winter here, yet," he observed, staring at the nearly naked trees lining the road.

"It isn't Halloween, yet," Annie pointed out, amused. "Did you expect to see snow on the ground?"

"I didn't know what to expect," he conceded. "When does it start snowing around here?"

"Real snow? Mid-December. We usually get some flurries before then, though."

He contemplated what she'd told him. In other circumstances, a chat about the weather would seem trivial, but Annie suspected that he was asking her about the climate because he needed to know what to expect once he moved to Connecticut. Getting used to the New England cold might be difficult for a native southern Californian like Keith. She wondered if he'd be able to make the adjustment.

Keith's ability to adjust to winter weather was the least of it, she admitted silently. The real question was whether he and Annie could adjust to being near each other on a daily basis, especially after all they'd been through.

"Do you have to work today?" he asked.

"No. I got someone to cover for me." Taking off from work on a Saturday morning added to Annie's sense of blithe irresponsibility. "How about you? How's that case you're assisting your friend with?"

"Complicated," he answered. "It's a class-action suit a group of women are bringing against their employer. They claim they were overlooked for promotions because they're women." He shook his head and chuckled. "I don't want to talk about it. I should be working on it this weekend, but I'm not. I'd just as soon not even think about it."

Keith seemed to be as happy as she was to abandon his responsibilities for the weekend. Annie shot him another brief look. His gaze remained forward and he slumped in the bucket seat, his long legs cramped in the space beneath the dashboard. "Are you tired?" she asked solicitously.

"Not really, no."

"Did you sleep on the plane?"

"No." He turned to her with an enigmatic smile—not a large one, but one which marked his cheeks with dimples. "I must have nodded off for a few minutes, just before we reached Chicago and I had to change planes. I remember a flight attendant jabbing me in the arm and yelling at me to fasten my seatbelt." His smile grew gentle, and his gaze intensified as he studied her. "You're so beautiful, Annie."

His compliment was unexpected—and unexpectedly blunt. She had spent a great deal of time that morning worrying about how she looked, pulling a variety of sweaters on and off until she settled on the soft pink cowl neck she had on, going through the same procedure with her slacks until she decided on her tailored gray corduroys, brushing her hair until she was certain that every strand glistened and every snarl had been eliminated, darkening her cheeks with a peach-hued blusher and then scrubbing it off. She had wanted to look beautiful for Keith. Now that she knew she'd been successful, she felt thrilled and humbled and momentarily tongue-tied.

"The past few days," he went on, his voice taking on a husky quality, "I kept wondering whether this was a hare-brained idea, flying out here like this, forgetting everything. Even on the plane... It seemed so crazy, Annie, just putting it all out of my mind—"

"Don't," she silenced him. This was not the time to re-hash all the things that had gone wrong between them. It was a time to celebrate what was right between them, and Annie didn't think that putting the rest out of their minds for a couple of days was crazy at all.

She let her eyes drift from the road to meet his. He gazed steadily at her, and his expression informed her that he understood why she'd cut him off. "I don't think it's crazy anymore," he reassured her. "The moment I saw you, I stopped thinking it was crazy."

The rest of the drive to Brenton passed in silence. Annie and Keith were lost in their own private thoughts—although Annie was positive their thoughts were pretty nearly identical. She was acutely aware of his warmth next to her, the dynamic strength of his body, the graceful shape of his large hands as they rested on his thighs. Running her tongue over her lips, she recaptured the lingering flavor of his kiss. Recalling how good it had felt to be held by him—imagining how good it would feel to be held by him again—Annie pressed her foot harder on the gas pedal, anxious to get home.

They remained silent as she coasted into the driveway and shut off the engine. Keith pulled his bag from the backseat, then jogged around the car to take Annie's hand. They strolled together up the front walk, which was almost completely buried beneath the season's final blizzard of leaves, and entered the house. Annie didn't let go of his hand until they'd reached her bedroom.

He scanned the room before entering. It was small but tastefully decorated, the furnishings modest so as not to overwhelm it. After surveying the maple dresser, the mirror with its matching maple frame, the cane rocker and the oval area rugs, which were distributed over the hardwood floor, his gaze came to rest on the double bed against one wall, which was dressed in a patchwork quilt and two plump down pillows.

After a minute, he lifted his eyes to Annie. His expression was transparent, his longing almost palpable. He dropped his bag to the floor and extended his arms to her.

Don't think, she warned herself. If this was crazy, so be it.

She crossed the room to him, and he folded his arms possessively around her. There was nothing polite about the kiss he gave her this time. It was hungry, greedy, devouring her with an eagerness that went well beyond what she'd sensed in him in his motel room the last time they'd been together. She suspected that his yearning for her didn't date back to that night at the motel, but instead had been building since he and Annie had ended their relationship. It was as if he'd been waiting for this moment, waiting for this kiss, ever since the day he'd left her six years ago.

No, she wasn't going to think about that. She wasn't going to think at all.

As her mouth fused with his, she slipped her hands under the flaps of his jacket and slid it off his shoulders. It fell to the floor behind him, and she went to work on his sweater, wedging her hands beneath the bottom edge and easing it up. When it bunched at his arms, he was forced to break from her long enough to remove it. He took advantage of the pause to strip off her sweater, as well.

He returned his mouth to hers as they continued undressing each other. Whenever they were forced to break the kiss it wasn't for long; as soon as one garment or another was shed, their mouths came together again, as if magnetized.

Finally they were both naked. Now that he had accomplished that essential task, Keith gathered Annie fully to him, and pressed her body to his. Her smooth, slim thighs touched his muscular, lightly haired ones; her breasts collided with his chest; her arms ringed his waist and her mouth reached the base of his neck. Her lips grazed against his Adam's apple and she felt it vibrate as he sighed.

"I came prepared," he whispered into her hair.

"I'm already prepared," she told him, her lips moving against his shoulder with each word.

His body responded to her remark in an obvious way, provoking a breathless moan from her. He loosened his hold on her only enough to enable them to cross the room to the bed. He helped her onto it and climbed on beside her. Propping himself up on his side, he peered down at her, brushing a few errant blond tresses back from her cheeks, then running his fingers to her throat, to the delicate line of her collarbone. "I love you, Annie," he whispered.

Don't think, her inner voice warned her once more. She wouldn't question the extent of his love, or meditate about what kind of love would drive a man to walk out on his woman when the going got rough. She wouldn't ask him if he was, perhaps, confusing love with lust. She would accept his words on faith. She would love him as much as he loved her, and she wouldn't analyze it further.

She rose to him, capturing his lips with hers and curling her hands around his shoulders to pull him down. He submitted willingly, sliding his tongue over hers, shifting his chest so that it rubbed against her breasts, stimulating her nipples. "Keith," she murmured dreamily, the single syllable filling his mouth.

His hands moved down her body. He caressed her breasts, the arching bones of her ribcage, the concave stretch of her belly, the feminine breadth of her hips. But he never lifted his mouth from hers. He wouldn't dare to kiss her breasts, she realized. He wouldn't dare to do anything that might spoil the magic by inviting bad memories.

She appreciated his consideration, but it wasn't necessary. She wanted him to kiss her everywhere. She wanted to feel his tongue against her skin, his lips conquering her flesh.

She wanted him to know that her body was totally his, that nothing was out of bounds, that bad memories no longer existed—at least not today.

Drawing her mouth from his, she inhaled raggedly. "Kiss me," she pleaded, rising higher on the pillow and cupping her hands around his cheeks. "Kiss me all over, Keith."

He lifted his head to view her. Evidently he read in her eyes the assurance he needed. He ran his hand up to her breast, rounded the soft swell, stroked it, shaped it to his palm. Then he bowed and took the nipple gently between his teeth.

She no longer had to tell herself not to think. His tender assault left her awash in sensations too strong to countenance anything as coherent as thought. She gripped his head, holding it to her, twining her fingers into the plush depths of his hair. His kiss unleashed her, sending daggers of longing deep into her. She wanted to describe to him the pleasure he was bringing her, but before she could shape the words he shifted his mouth to the other breast, inflaming it with his lips and tongue before drawing it deep into his mouth. She moaned something incoherent and hoped he understood.

Her hips twisted on the bed, uncomfortable from the deluge of aching need Keith had released within her. She reached down, her fingers moving across his abdomen, seeking. When she found him, his entire body lurched and he groaned. He pulled back from her and let his eyes meet hers again. "I'm so ready for you," he mumbled, his voice rasping brokenly.

"I'm ready for you, too," she responded.

Apparently he didn't believe her. He glided his hand down her body to the golden triangle of hair between her thighs, to the moist flesh below. He moved against her and she arched reflexively, closing her eyes, feeling for a moment that this alone would be enough to satisfy her.

"Oh, Annie," he whispered, deepening his caress for a moment, awed by her overwhelming response. "Annie..."

When he took his hand away, she bit back a protest. It wouldn't be for long, she knew. Soon he would be with her completely. Opening her eyes, she watched as he poised himself above her, as he lowered his lips and his body to hers. He began slowly, but then, overcome, he plunged hard and deep, causing her body to tighten around him, bringing tears to her eyes.

He froze, fighting for breath, watching her with concern. "I'm hurting you," he murmured, withdrawing.

"No." She clamped her hands onto his hips and held him inside her. Gradually her body relaxed around him, growing accustomed to this miraculous invasion, savoring it, wanting more.

He rocked her, his thrusts sure and gentle, stroking her soul as his hands had stroked her body. She adopted his rhythm, rising up to him and then sinking, rising and sinking as it all came back to her, the strangeness and familiarity of it, the wonder of it, the ecstasy. Six years was a long time, but her body remembered. She remembered what Keith had done to her, what he could do, what he was doing to her with his love.

Memory was replaced by what she was experiencing now. The growing heat was real, the nearly unbearable tension, the abrupt explosion tearing her apart, pounding through her, paradoxically shattering and soothing her in blissful aftershocks. This was real, the present. This was love. This was Keith.

She clung to him until the final tremors faded, leaving her tranquil and sated and scarcely able to move. She had been so transported by the glory of it that she'd hardly been aware of Keith's equally shattering climax. He settled onto her with a harsh gasp, his eyes closed and his skin damp. In spite of the streaks of silver in his hair, in spite of the lines at the corners of his eyes and the pale shadow of beard along his jaw, he looked like a little boy to her, his lashes thick and dark against his cheeks, his lips parted slightly as he wrestled with his breath. She closed her arms protectively around him and replayed in her mind the sound of his voice whispering, "I love you, Annie."

She loved him, too. Nothing else mattered. Nothing else existed. All she knew, all she had, was her love for Keith, and his for her.

His eyes fluttered open and he leaned back so that he could see her. A faint crease marked the bridge of his nose as he perused her face, and he flexed his mouth several times before speaking. "Are you all right?"

She lifted her finger to his lower lip and traced it, trying to soften it into a smile. "I'm a lot better than just all right," she told him.

"I thought...when we started, you were so..." He broke off, but his gaze remained on her, searching for reassurance.

"It was wonderful, Keith."

He appeared unconvinced.

She stroked his lip again, then let her hand drop to the bed. She knew he'd keep pestering her until she told him the truth. "It's just that ... If I seemed a little tense at first, it's only because I haven't been with anyone in a long time."

Something sharpened in his eyes, a glint of suspicion. "How long?" he asked.

Annie rolled away, preferring to present him with her back while she sorted through her thoughts. If she told him the whole truth, that she hadn't had a lover since he'd left, how would he take it? Would he be unduly flattered? Would he be disturbed? Would he think there was something wrong with her?

Before she could tell him anything, he guessed. "Six years?"

She nodded.

He didn't say anything for a minute. His fingers floated over the contours of her back, the undulating line of her spine, the crests of her shoulder blades, the two tiny dimples on the small of her back. "Don't be embarrassed," he finally said.

"I'm not," Annie mumbled.

"Then look at me." He rolled her back, urging her onto her side so that she was facing him, sharing his pillow. "Your way might have been better," he pointed out, smiling ironically. "I kept looking for something as good as what we had, and I never found it. You didn't waste your time looking."

"That wasn't why I haven't been with anyone else," Annie argued. "Believe me, if I'd ever lived anywhere where there was a reasonable population of decent men—"

"Oh yeah?" Keith snorted skeptically. "Like graduate school, for instance? UConn's a big school. I'm sure there were men there. And in Portland. Even here, in Brenton. Annie, you're an incredibly attractive woman. If you ever let on that you were available, you'd have to fight the men off."

"You're saying it's my fault nobody's come on to me?"

"I'm saying it's your doing. Not your fault."

Annie scowled. "I bet that does your ego a world of good," she grunted before rolling away again.

She felt him lifting her hair away from her shoulders and pressing his lips to the nape of her neck. "I love you," he said. And those simple words managed to vanquish her chagrin. "I want to love you again. Help me."

He circled her wrist with his fingers and eased her onto her back. Then he guided her hand to him. Judging by his aroused state, he didn't need much help from her, but she touched him tenderly, playing her fingers over his length, feeling him press against her palm. He touched her as well, his fingers awakening her as she awakened him, until she was desperate for him again, desperately aware of the emptiness inside her, anxious for him to fill it.

He did. This time he had more control. He varied his tempo, keeping his eyes open so that he could watch Annie's reactions as he felt them, so that he could see in her eyes the joy he was bringing her.

She had more control, as well. She drew her legs up and around him, taking him deeper into her, offering him more. She watched him as he watched her, noting the strain in his strong features, the glazed look in his eyes, the tension in his jaw. She wanted to know everything his body was undergoing. She wanted to know the exact instant he reached his release, the precise moment she delivered him to heaven.

It wasn't easy, for the simple reason that he sent her there first, drawing her awareness away from him to center on herself, on the place deep inside her where love expressed itself most intimately. And then he was there with her, reaching his own definition of intimacy. The boundary separating his existence from hers blurred, grew indistinct, vanished altogether in a blaze of love.

Afterward, Keith lay across Annie, his body heavy, his energy spent. She combed her fingers through his hair again and again, listening to his shallow breathing and feeling his heart race against her. Eventually, his pulse slowed, his respiration deepened, and his body grew even heavier.

She wiggled out from under him. He mumbled something and turned over. It didn't take long for Annie to realize that he'd fallen asleep.

Smiling, she sat up, folded back the quilt, and shoved his body around on the bed until she was able to cover him. Without waking, he punched the pillow beneath his head and nestled deeper into it. Annie kissed his cheek, then climbed off the bed. The combination of jet lag and lovemaking was clearly too much for him. He'd be out for a while.

She didn't have to worry about disturbing his rest, but even so, she tiptoed across the room to her closet, pulled out her bathrobe, and left the bedroom for the bathroom. After a quick shower, she stole back into the bedroom to dress. Once she'd finished dressing and brushing her hair, she turned toward the bed. Keith hadn't budged.

She left the bedroom again, quietly closing the door behind her. It was nearly lunchtime, and although she wasn't hungry, she knew she ought to force something down her throat. Too excited to eat earlier that morning, she had skipped breakfast. She couldn't skip lunch, too.

She poured herself a glass of milk and nibbled on a cookie. While she ate, she gazed through the window at the backyard. The sun was overhead, so her stained-glass ornaments didn't spill their colors onto the wall. They looked lifeless to her, the lead bumpy in spots, the glass mottled. They were clearly the work of an amateur. She remembered making them in an effort to recover from her depression. She might as well have taken up basket weaving or finger painting.

She turned swiftly from the window, refusing to think about the situation that had led to her flight to Teri's home, and to Teri's dragging Annie to a friend's stained glass workshop. Once Keith was back in California, Annie could think about that all she wanted. But not today.

After rinsing out her glass, she stole down the hall to her bedroom to check on Keith. She entered, hovered over the bed long enough to make sure he was still breathing and then slipped out again.

He reached for her and felt only air. Startled, he opened his eyes. They focused on the alarm clock on her night table: three-thirty. He was alone.

Groaning, he sat up and gazed around the room. Annie's room, in Annie's house. He hadn't dreamed the whole thing.

If his having come here wasn't a dream, he pondered, then the rest couldn't have been a dream, either. He hadn't dreamed that he'd made love to Annie. He hadn't dreamed her kisses, her passion, the magnificent warmth of her body enveloping his, absorbing him, making him hers.

Nor had he dreamed the part about her telling him she'd been alone for six years.

He drew his knees up to his chest, folded his arms across them, rested his chin on his forearms and meditated. It seemed incomprehensible to him that Annie would have gone without male companionship for so long. Not just because her beauty would have attracted men to her, but because she was so vibrantly sensual. Or she had been, when they'd been living together. As often as not, she had initiated their lovemaking. Part of what had made him adore her was her appetite, her energy—her downright sexiness.

Six years? Six years of celibacy? He couldn't believe it—except that Annie would never lie about such a thing. And even if she had lied, her body had given her away.

He felt guilty for having known other women when Annie hadn't known other men. He felt guilty for having wounded her so badly that she had renounced her own sexuality. But mixed in with the guilt was a totally unjustifiable anger. He understood that Annie had avoided other men not because she loved Keith but because she'd been scarred by him. It hadn't been an act of faithfulness or loyalty on her part. It had been an act of rejection.

Don't. He heard her voice shaping that one word, a quiet command. She had said it in the car when he'd told her he thought it was crazy to forget everything that was wrong between them. The admonition remained with him: *Don't* think about the past, *don't* ruin this weekend. *Don't* spoil the dream.

Only it wasn't a dream. He hadn't dreamed it. He was here.

Annie was here, somewhere, too. Keith gathered his clothing from the floor and left the bedroom in search of a bathroom. Once he was washed and dressed, he set out to find Annie. Entering the kitchen, he spotted her through the window, out in the backyard, raking leaves. She was wielding her rake near the hedge that separated her yard from her next door neighbor's, and she appeared engrossed in her labor.

He returned to the bedroom for his jacket, slipped it on and went out the kitchen door to join her. She had accumulated the brown leaves in a huge heap—an enormously tempting heap. Unable to resist, Keith raced across the lawn to the pile and dived into it, scattering leaves everywhere.

Annie shrieked, more in surprise than annoyance. "You creep!" she cried, dropping her rake and storming across the lawn to the demolished mound of leaves. When Keith rolled onto his back he found her glowering down at him, her hands on her hips and her feet several inches from his nose. "You scared me! And look what you've done—that's two hours worth of work you've just destroyed!"

In response, Keith grabbed her ankle and gave it a sharp tug, causing her to lose her balance and tumble down to the ground next to him. "Hey, I'm a California boy," he justified himself. "What do I know about dead leaves?"

"You're about to learn," Annie huffed, though she was laughing. "I'm going to make you clean this mess up."

"If it's my mess," Keith countered, dazzled by the rosy glow of her cheeks, the bright blue of her eyes, the glorious length of her sun-colored hair, "then I can do whatever I damned well want with it." He shifted his weight, easily pinning her onto her back, and straddled her waist. "Now

I've got you where I want you," he threatened in his most villainous tone.

Unimpressed, Annie wrinkled her nose. "I think I liked you better when you were asleep."

"Too bad, Annie. Now I'm well rested, and you're totally at my mercy." He leaned down and peppered her face with kisses. "Let's shock your neighbors," he whispered, blanketing her body with his and moving his hips suggestively against hers.

"I'll tell you who's shocked," Annie reproached him, although she was too breathless to sound stern. "I'm shocked that an old codger like you has so much energy."

"Old codger!" Keith roared.

"You're going gray," Annie reminded him.

"I'm going silver," he countered, "and it's a sign of distinction, not age. I happen to be just entering my prime."

"Well," Annie said, smiling slyly, "if you're so young and prime, Keith, let's see you rake up these leaves. It'll be good practice for when you move here."

Keith's eyes locked onto hers, and both their smiles vanished, all playfulness gone. *Here?* What did that simple word mean? Did she want him to move *here*, to her house? Was this an invitation?

They hadn't discussed where he'd live once he moved to Brenton. In his fantasies he lived with Annie, but he had no idea whether she shared that dream. "Do you want raking the leaves to be my chore?" he asked cautiously.

Annie held his gaze for a second more, then turned away. "Let's not talk about it, Keith," she said quickly, sliding out from under him and pushing herself up to sit.

Several twigs and brown leaves were tangled in her hair. Keith wondered whether she'd recoil if he touched her—she looked so tense. He lifted his hand to her head and unraveled the stem of a perfectly shaped oak leaf, careful not to yank her hair in the process. When she didn't tell him to stop, he pressed his luck. "When can we talk about it?"

"Not now."

"I want to live with you," he said. If he hadn't already reached that conclusion, the morning he'd spent in Annie's arms would have convinced him. Making love with her had been spectacular, and he wanted to be able to do it again, every day. He wanted to be with her, even if they weren't making love. He wanted to rake her leaves and sleep with her and wake up to her. Although he'd spent many years waking up alone, when he'd done it a half hour ago he'd felt bereft. Once he had Annie, he didn't want to lose her.

"Not now," she repeated, more firmly. She tugged most of the other bits of vegetation from her long hair before Keith could help her, then stood and dusted off her slacks. "The rake is over there," she said coolly, pointing across the yard. "There are some trash bags on the back porch. I'll be in the kitchen if you need me."

I need you now, Keith almost called after her. But he held his silence. He watched her walk across the grass to the porch and enter the house through the kitchen door.

If he'd told her he needed her, she might have thought he meant that he needed her assistance in raking the leaves. Or else, she might have thought the truth—that he needed her to help him work out this latest problem, to help him surmount this new hurdle. He needed her in his life.

Don't, her voice came back to him again. Maybe she was right. Maybe now wasn't the time. Although Keith couldn't imagine that the important issues would be easier to solve long-distance over the phone, he had to honor Annie's wishes and avoid them this weekend.

So he raked. He raked all the leaves he'd scattered, and the leaves that had gotten trapped beneath the hedge. Then he went to the back porch to get a trash bag from the box Annie had left there. As he neared the porch, he glanced toward the kitchen window and saw her. Her head was bowed; she was probably washing something in the sink. Her hair hung like a yellow frame around her face, illuminated by the overhead kitchen light, and her expression was unreadable.

Keith wondered what she was thinking about: the breathtaking love they'd shared that morning? Keith's desire to live with her?

Or Adam, the biggest "don't" of the weekend, the one subject they still hadn't found the courage to face?

Nine

"This is delicious," Keith said after tasting a piece of meat. "What is it?"

Annie gazed at him across the kitchen table. The house had a dining room, but since she lived alone she hadn't bothered to buy a dining-room table. On the rare occasions she entertained, her style was generally casual—cheese and crackers or platters of sandwiches served on the coffee table in the living room. She never hosted anything as formal as a sit-down dinner.

"It's a stew I concocted," she answered. "Beef, onions, broccoli, soya sauce and a splash of vermouth." Her voice floated calmly into the air, not revealing the merest hint of what she was thinking.

What she was thinking—what she was afraid to admit to Keith—was that she felt unreasonably comfortable eating dinner with him here in her kitchen. She loved having him to look at while she ate, and having him to talk to, even on a subject as inane as the ingredients in her stew. It wasn't just loneliness that made her treasure his company so much. When she and Keith had lived together, she had adored the day-in-day-out of it, the constant knowledge that he was around. She still adored it.

But to have him move in with her... She wasn't ready for that. Just because she and Keith were still good together in bed didn't mean she wanted to set up house with him all over again.

Still good in bed? She groaned inwardly at that paltry description. What had happened between her and Keith that morning transcended words. It had been emotionally cataclysmic, spiritually wrenching.

She had loved Keith in bed that morning. She had given him not just her body but her heart, her mind, her soul, her very essence. She had loved him simply for what he was at that moment, not for who he used to be or what he'd meant to her in the past.

She wished that she'd been able to hang onto that glorious, heedless love. But the minute Keith had said he wanted to live with her, he'd unlatched the floodgate and reality had come spilling through, reminding her of everything else. Suddenly, she could no longer think of him only as who he was now. They'd lived together in the past, after all, and they'd hurt each other and hated each other. No matter what had happened in Annie's bed that morning, certain facts couldn't be refuted.

"I don't want to be rushed into anything," she announced, giving voice to her troubling thoughts.

Keith's fork froze in midair. "I beg your pardon?"

"First you say you want to move to Brenton, and then you say you want to move into my home..."

He accepted the abrupt change of topic with a small sigh. "Annie, do you think I'd want to move to Brenton if you *didn't* have a home here?"

"All I'm saying is, I don't want to be rushed. You're asking a lot of me, Keith."

"No more than I'm asking of myself," he maintained. "I'm asking you to forgive me—but I'm also asking myself to forgive you. Believe me, Annie, I know just how tall an order that is."

Annie set down her silverware and concentrated on the glass of ice water she'd fixed for herself. She studied the melting ice cubes, feeling something resembling ice cubes inside herself, cold and shrinking, leaving behind a chilly pool of guilt. Then she lifted the glass and sipped, hoping the water would wash the image away. She honestly didn't believe she'd done anything to Keith as horrible as what he'd done to her... but what difference did that make? Obviously, Keith was having as much difficulty forgiving her as she was having forgiving him.

"Given that we really botched things badly last time," Annie commented quietly, "what makes you think we won't botch things this time?"

"Maybe we've grown up," Keith suggested. "Maybe we've learned from our mistakes."

Annie took another long sip of water to keep herself from blurting out that the biggest mistake she'd ever made had been to rely on Keith—to rely on their love. Love was supposed to bring people closer in the face of tragedy. Whatever Keith and Annie had back then, it had driven them apart.

If it was love, then it was nothing more than the love she and Keith had found that morning, a love born of passion, not trust. Probably that was all they'd ever had. No wonder it hadn't been enough to keep them together.

But they would have that kind of love again tonight, Annie resolved. Keith was leaving the following afternoon. They weren't about to learn how to forgive each other in the next eighteen hours. They might as well spend those hours giving each other whatever they were able to give. For all Annie knew, she and Keith were doomed never to know the other kind of love, the trusting kind.

She smiled faintly. There were worse fates in life than to spend a night with a man you loved, even if the love wasn't powerful enough to vanquish everything that stood in its path. If Annie had learned anything from her mistakes, it was that she shouldn't expect too much from anyone else, or from love.

"Would you like some dessert?" she asked, glimpsing his nearly empty plate. "I've got some ice cream in the freezer."

"No, thanks."

"Coffee?"

Before Keith could answer, the doorbell rang. Annie was oddly relieved. The strange dance she and Keith were performing, tiptoeing around certain topics, trespassing on something significant and then hastily retreating to safe talk about stews and desserts, was tiring. How had they managed to talk so easily six years ago? she wondered. What had they talked about then? Stews and desserts, no doubt. But it hadn't been such a strain back then, because they hadn't had to work so hard to avoid the important issues.

If they couldn't talk about the important issues now, Annie conceded, it was just as well that someone had dropped by to divert them for a while.

Keith rose when Annie did, partly, she suspected, out of courtesy and partly out of curiosity. He followed her into the living room, where he waited while she crossed to the front door and opened it.

Justine Willis was standing on the front porch. She had on a pair of blue jeans, a zippered parka and sneakers. Her hair surrounded her upturned face in unruly brown tufts. A small fabric-covered suitcase stood on the porch at her feet. "Hey, Annie!" she hollered, with the same gusto she exhibited whenever she arrived at the library.

Annie gaped at Justine. How had the little girl figured out where Annie lived? How had she gotten here? And why had she brought a suitcase with her?

"Can I come in?" Justine asked, skewing her mouth into an entreating smile.

Annie hesitated. She couldn't very well slam her door on the girl. On the other hand, there was the suitcase.

"What are you doing, Justine?" Annie questioned. "What is that suitcase for?"

"It's just got some stuff in it," Justine said placidly, lifting the bag by its plastic handle and hoisting it over the threshold ahead of herself.

Annie reluctantly stepped aside, permitting Justine to enter. "What stuff?" she asked, dreading the answer.

Justine's reply fulfilled her worst fears. "Just some stuff I need. I'm running away from home, Annie," she reported solemnly. "I'm sort of hoping you'll let me stay here."

"Stay here? In my house, you mean?"

Justine didn't bother to elaborate on her plans. Her gaze had fastened itself to Keith, and her smile widened. "Hey, I know you! You're the man that named the bird in the library Mr. Chips! What's your name again? I think you told me, but I forgot."

"Keith LaMotte," he said, shooting Annie a bemused glance.

"You remember Justine Willis, don't you?" Annie mumbled, shutting the door and then leaning against it, using the time to take stock of the situation. What was so special about this humble shingled house that made everyone want to move into it, all of a sudden? "Justine, I'm not sure what you're doing here, but—"

"I just *told* you, Annie. I'm running away from home. This is a real nice place, Annie," she said, giving the living room a critical once-over before wandering into the kitchen.

Annie chased after Justine, astonished by the girl's audacity. She found Justine standing in the center of the kitchen, oblivious to the dinner dishes on the table as she studied the array of stained-glass figures hanging in front of the window above the sink. Because the evening sky was rapidly dimming to darkness, no light passed through the tinted panels of the ornaments, but Justine seemed to find them spellbinding.

"Wow! Those are neat!" Justine exclaimed as she unzipped her parka. "I'm going to like it here, Annie, I know it." She pulled the parka off and flung it toward the counter.

"Justine." Annie caught the jacket in midair and draped it over the back of a chair. "You can't stay here. You've got your own house. This house is mine."

"It looks big enough to me," Justine declared, swinging open the refrigerator and inspecting its contents. "I won't eat much, and I'll sleep on the couch if you want. I don't mind. You won't even know I'm here."

Fat chance of that, Annie muttered silently. Justine's voice was so strident, Annie's neighbors were probably aware of her presence on the block. One thing Justine Willis was not was inconspicuous.

"Justine," Annie said, using her sternest librarian voice, "I'm still not sure I understand why you came here. But in any case, you can't run away from home."

Justine spun around nimbly and confronted Annie with a stare as piercing as her voice. "How come?"

"Because... because I'm sure your parents are very worried about you," Annie pointed out.

"No, they're not. Can I have a glass of milk?"

"Justine, listen to me," Annie demanded, planting her hands on her hips and bearing down on the little girl. "Your parents *are* worried. They're probably frantic." Justine's incredulous expression compelled Annie to add, "If I were your mother, I'd be frantic."

"Yeah," Justine agreed wholeheartedly. "That's why I'm here. You care about me more than my mother does. She doesn't care that I'm gone, Annie. Honest. I bet she hasn't even noticed I'm not home."

Annie had met Madelyn Willis on only a few occasions, and their conversations hadn't amounted to much. But, no matter how irresponsibly the woman behaved by regularly stranding her daughter with Annie at the library, Annie couldn't imagine Justine's mother failing to notice that her daughter had left home.

Annie had been a mother once. She knew the way mothers felt about their children.

She decided to take a gentler tack. "Justine," she said, approaching the girl and squatting down to her eye level. "Whatever happened at home, I'm sure your mother wants you back. If you had a fight with her, if you were naughty and she punished you . . . whatever it was, it's not so serious that you've got to run away."

Justine looked nonplussed. "We didn't have a fight, Annie. It's nothing like that. Can I have a glass of milk?"

Annie assessed the situation. If she didn't give Justine a drink, the little girl would likely continue asking for one and not listen to anything Annie said. Sighing, she stood, pulled a carton of milk from the refrigerator and filled a glass. When she turned to give the milk to Justine, Annie's eyes met Keith's. He was lounging in the doorway, watching the interchange between Annie and Justine. As soon as he had Annie's attention, he motioned his head in a quick nod.

She understood the gesture: he wanted her to leave the kitchen with him. She'd lived with Keith long enough for them to be able to communicate without words. "Here," she said, presenting Justine with the glass. "I'll be right back."

Annie joined Keith in the doorway. He took her elbow and ushered her into the living room. "I think you ought to call the police," he whispered.

"What?" Annie nearly laughed at the absurdity of his suggestion. Brenton was a small town; it wasn't as if Justine had traveled to some strange city halfway across the country. Certainly Annie would be able to talk some sense

into her and get her back home without dragging the police
into it.

"Annie, the kid's a runaway. Call the police and let them
handle it."

"Don't be silly," she scolded him. "This isn't a kid, it's
Justine. I know her and she knows me. I'm sure we can
straighten the whole thing out."

"It's not your business to straighten the whole thing out,"
Keith murmured. "Call the police."

"I will not," Annie declared firmly. "There's no need."
She pivoted and marched back into the kitchen, shaking her
head in surprise that Keith could take such a hard-line attitude toward what was probably no more than a minor
squabble between Justine and her mother.

Justine had finished her milk and was rummaging in a
drawer. For a horrified moment, Annie wondered whether
the little girl planned to rob her. Her paranoia was undoubtedly a result of Keith's having mentioned the police,
and she shook it off with a shrug before asking, "What are
you looking for, Justine?"

"Some cookies or something. I'm starving, Annie. I forgot to fix myself any dinner before I left."

"Didn't your mother make you dinner?"

"Uh-uh." Justine tugged open another drawer, but Annie interceded before she could paw through it. She slid the
drawer shut with her hip and produced a box of cookies
from a cabinet above the counter.

"Why didn't your mother make you any dinner?" she
asked after handing three cookies to Justine.

Justine wolfed one of the cookies down before replying.
"She was too busy."

"Too busy to make you your dinner?"

"That's right." Justine gobbled up the other two cookies. "See, she prob'ly still hasn't noticed I'm gone. She
doesn't care about me anyway, Annie. Please, can't I stay
with you?" She peered up at Annie, her gaze so imploring

that Annie temporarily forgave her for barging in and going through the kitchen drawers.

"Here," Annie said, getting a clean plate and serving up some of the remaining stew for Justine. She cleared a space at the table and led the child to a chair. "Why don't you eat this?"

"Hey, that's pretty funny," Justine observed. "First dessert and then dinner. Kind of backward, huh, Annie?"

"Consider it a special treat." Annie brought a napkin and a fork to the table, then patted Justine on the head. "I'll be back in a few minutes."

She left the kitchen and started down the hall to the bedroom, resolved that she would call Madelyn Willis and tell her where her daughter was—and maybe criticize her for her failure to feed her daughter. Keith intercepted Annie outside the bedroom. "Are you going to call the police?" he asked.

"You sound like a broken record," Annie mocked. "Of course I'm not going to call the police. I'm going to call Justine's mother and tell her to come and pick up her daughter."

"And if her mother isn't home?" Keith posed.

Annie frowned. Why on earth was he playing guessing games with her? If Justine's mother wasn't home, Annie would speak to Justine's father. If neither was home, she'd wait a while and call again. Or she'd ask Justine where she lived, and drive her home herself.

"What I'm trying to say, Annie, is that maybe Justine left home for a good reason," Keith explained in a gentle voice.

Annie gave him a blank stare. "What do you mean, a good reason?"

"She said her mother wouldn't even miss her. Maybe she's telling the truth."

Annie still didn't understand what Keith was getting at. "All right, so maybe her parents went out for dinner and left her home without a baby-sitter. That doesn't mean she's supposed to run away."

"Annie." Keith's dark gray eyes bore into her, solemn and steady. "Annie, all I'm saying is, maybe there's a . . . a problem at Justine's house."

"A problem?"

"There are lots of possibilities," Keith said delicately. "I'm a lawyer, and as a lawyer, I'm advising you not to get in the middle of it. Call the police and let them take care of it."

Annie stared at him. Did he think Justine was the victim of some sort of abuse? Did he think she'd run away because she feared for her life? "This is Brenton, not Los Angeles," she reminded him. "I think I know what you're implying, Keith, and I can assure you, those sorts of things don't happen here."

"Don't kid yourself," he said dryly. "They happen everywhere." His manner softening, he continued. "I'm probably wrong. It's likely that nothing all that bad has happened to Justine. Probably her parents are frantically looking for her right now, just like you told her. But the wisest move would be to call the police and let them get Justine and her parents back together again. Okay?"

Annie pondered Keith's suggestion She hated the notion of calling the police about something as trivial as a little girl's quarrel with her mother. But Keith was a lawyer; maybe his advice made sense.

What if she were still a mother? Closing her eyes, Annie tried to picture Adam at Justine's age—close to the age he'd be now if he had lived. She tried to imagine his running away, and then her reaction. Of course she wouldn't care who called whom; she wouldn't care whether or not the police were a part of it. All she would care about was getting her son back, safe and sound.

"I'll call the police," she relented, entering her bedroom and crossing to the bed.

She lifted the telephone directory from her night table shelf, flipped through it until she found the listing, and dialed. The desk sergeant with whom she spoke took her name and address, as well as Justine's name, and promised that an officer would come over to her house. When Annie hung up and glanced toward the hallway, she saw that Keith had disappeared.

Her solitude gave her a moment to think. This was definitely not the way she had expected her evening with Keith to proceed. She'd expected that they would have coffee, skirt around various taboo subjects, and then retire to bed, where, for a while, they could forget everything but their passion for each other. She hadn't expected that Justine Willis would appear on her doorstep, begging for shelter. Nor had she expected that she and Keith would argue over what to do about it.

He'd called the police the morning Adam had died, too. Annie had gone into shock, and Keith had taken charge and called the police.

She hadn't gone into shock over Justine's intrusion, but perhaps she'd been addled and overly protective. Keith had been logical and calm in urging her to summon the police. That was his solution to all crises: logic. Calm. A lack of emotion. He detached himself and took care of everything.

As much as Annie respected the rationality of Keith's approach, she resented the hell out of it.

Groaning at the miserable memories creeping up on her, she hoisted herself up and stalked out of the bedroom. From the kitchen doorway, she spied on Keith as he kept Justine company at the table. He was nibbling a cookie from the box Annie had left on the counter and chatting with Justine. "So the guy visits these three witches, and they're cooking up this really disgusting soup, with newt eyes and frog toes and stuff like that—"

"Keith!" Annie hurried into the room and gave Justine a quick perusal. The little girl's eyes were round, her expression rapt as she listened to the story Keith was narrating. "I think," Annie reproached him, "that Justine's a little too young for *Macbeth*."

"Well, she requested 'Sophie the Dragon,' but I don't know it," Keith explained. "That's your story."

"Would you tell it to me?" Justine asked, evidently willing to leave Keith's version of *Macbeth* unfinished for now.

Annie eyed Keith. He was watching her, his face inscrutable. She couldn't very well tell him, in front of Justine, that she'd done as she'd promised and phoned the police. He didn't need a report, anyway. He was undoubtedly sure she'd obeyed him. He was the one in charge of things, after all.

Ignoring the fresh twinge of resentment she suffered at the thought, Annie turned back to Justine and rested her hips against the counter. Justine's plate was empty, and Keith had apparently refilled her milk glass. The poor child must have been ravenous. And her life was about to be invaded by police officers. The least she deserved was "Sophie the Dragon."

"All right," Annie acquiesced. "Once upon a time, there was a dragon named Sophie..." She told Justine about the rainbow-colored smoke that poured from Sophie's nostrils, and the fear Sophie induced in human beings. She told Justine about how, gradually, the human beings came to appreciate the rainbow colors so much, they stopped being afraid of the smoke, and how, if people and dragons overcome their differences, they could learn to live with each other, happily ever after.

The doorbell rang again. Before Annie could push away from the counter, Keith was out of his seat. "I'll get it," he said firmly, leaving no room for debate.

Annie seethed. She'd thought Justine was presumptuous, but Keith was ten times as presumptuous, answering Annie's door as if he lived here. Which, of course, was exactly what he wanted, and exactly what she was resisting.

She heard voices out in the living room. Then Madelyn Willis dashed into the kitchen. "Justine!" she shrieked, swooping down on her daughter and enveloping her in a smothering hug. "Oh, my god! Justine! Are you all right?"

Annie decided to give the mother and daughter some privacy. Madelyn was too engrossed in her child even to notice Annie's polite smile. She left the kitchen.

Keith and a uniformed policeman stood in the living room, talking softly. They fell silent at Annie's entrance, and then the policeman addressed her. "Miss Jameson? Thanks for calling us. Mrs. Willis was quite beside herself, worrying about her little girl."

"Oh. That's good, I guess." She lifted her eyes to Keith's, sharing with him another tacit communication. Obviously, his worst fears about what might have motivated Justine's flight from home were unfounded. Her mother *had* missed her and was eager to bring her home again.

"And I appreciate your calling the police instead of trying to take care of this yourself," the officer went on. "That was a smart move, Miss Jameson. We're better equipped to deal with these domestic problems."

Annie bristled. "Yes, well, that was Keith's idea, not mine," she said shortly. She hoped he wouldn't get smug about the policeman's praise. He hadn't been smug when Adam had died, but he'd mastered the situation and taken care of everything in the proper fashion. Just like now.

"Well," the policeman said, heading for the kitchen. "If you'll excuse me, I'd like to talk to the child now."

Annie braced herself, waiting for Keith to serenade her with I-told-you-so's. But all he said was, "I like that dragon story. You ought to write it down."

"What for?" she asked with a startled laugh. Her story about Sophie was the last thing she'd expected Keith to mention.

"So you'll never forget it," he answered. "You ought to preserve it so it won't be forgotten. Maybe you'll need it someday."

Someday, if she ever had a child of her own. Annie intuitively knew that was what Keith was thinking.

She didn't speak. Keith's gaze held hers, and she detected in the smoky depths of his eyes a glimmer of emotion. He had no emotional attachment to Justine Willis, so the emotion must have resulted from thoughts of Annie's child—and his. Maybe he wasn't as much in control as he pretended to be.

Madelyn Willis appeared in the living room, interrupting Annie's ruminations. "The police officer wants a few minutes alone with Justine," she explained, running her fingers through the chic curls of her hair and smiling nervously. "Annie, I'm so sorry Justine bothered you. I know she's very fond of you. I hope she didn't spoil your evening."

"Of course she didn't," Annie assured Madelyn, although she wasn't sure she was speaking the truth.

"I mean, here you are, enjoying a nice, quiet dinner with your friend—"she cast Keith a hesitant smile "—and suddenly, there's my little girl on your doorstep—"

"It was no problem," Annie insisted. "Really." Madelyn seemed distraught enough about her daughter's disappearance. She shouldn't be fretting over whether or not Justine had ruined Annie and Keith's dinner.

Madelyn shot Keith another edgy smile, and he took that as his cue to leave. He was a stranger, after all, an outsider, and he had the good grace to leave the two women alone. "Excuse me, please," he mumbled before sauntering down the hall to the bedroom.

Madelyn watched his departure, then turned fully to Annie. "I'm sure Justine did this to get attention," she confided anxiously. "And I can't say I blame her. I love my little girl, but lately, I just haven't been able to give her the attention she deserves."

"Oh." Annie didn't want to be made privy to the dynamics of Madelyn's relationship with her daughter, and she almost envied Keith for leaving the room while she was trapped listening to Madelyn bare her soul. But Madelyn seemed to need to talk and Annie obliged by listening.

"It's just, my life is such a mess these days," Madelyn went on. "My husband's asked me for a divorce. I've been trying to work it out with him, to convince him that the whole thing's a big mistake. I've been getting my hair done, and I lost some weight, and... and it's been hard on me. I love Justine, I love her so much. I ought to have paid more attention to her and told Carl to go to hell. She's the one who ought to be getting all my attention."

Annie made what she hoped was a reassuring murmur in response.

"But you know, you get so wrapped up in your own problems sometimes.... I just thought, Justine can take care of herself until I get things settled with Carl. It never occurred to me that this divorce is tearing her life apart, too. I was trying so hard to avoid the divorce, and now look. Justine's telling me, in her own way, that I'm not giving her enough love." Madelyn dabbed at the tears that were forming in her eyes.

Annie gave Madelyn's shoulder a warm squeeze. "I'm sure it'll all work out," she said, wondering what gave her the right to make such a claim. "You and Justine need to sit down and talk things over. I'm sure she knows you love her."

"People don't automatically know that," Madelyn said with a conviction that seemed born of experience. "And it's not enough to tell them. You've got to show them. I'll just have to show Justine."

The policeman and Justine entered the living room. "I'm ready to come home now," she said sheepishly, glancing at her mother and then lowering her eyes.

Madelyn wrapped her in a crushing hug. "I want you home, Justine," she whispered. "Please forgive Mommy for being so distracted. It won't happen ever again. I love you."

A few minutes later, the Willises and the policeman departed. It took Annie a moment to adjust to the sudden calm, and to the realization that she and Keith were once again alone, faced with each other and their own unresolved problems. She locked the door, then surveyed the living room, the empty dining area, the imprints left on the carpet by Madelyn's high-heeled shoes and Justine's tread-soled sneakers.

Every family has its tragedies, she pondered with a heavy sigh.

Depressed by the thought, she went to the kitchen to clean up the dinner dishes. Keith arrived in the kitchen shortly after her. She gathered the plates from the table, carried them to the sink, washed them and then stacked them in the rack to dry. Keith put away the milk and cookies, then sponged off the table. Neither of them spoke until the room was tidy.

"Strange evening," he said.

Annie grinned crookedly. "Even if Justine hadn't barged in on us, it would have been strange. Having you here is strange."

Keith seemed able to understand her unspoken message. "In time it won't be," he said. "At least, I hope it won't be."

"Keith..." Annie dried her hands, hung the dish towel on a hook and turned to him. She studied him carefully, noting the still unfamiliar silver strands in his hair, the determined set of his chin, the sensual thinness of his lips, and finally his eyes, the color and hardness of flint. "Were you completely in control the day Adam died?" she asked.

He opened his mouth to answer, then thought again and pressed his lips together. His eyes grew distant and a muscle fluttered in his jaw. When his focus returned to Annie again, he gave her an enigmatic smile. "That's off-limits, Annie."

"But—"

"You set the ground rules for this weekend," he reminded her, moving across the room and pulling her into his arms. "We'll talk about it some other time."

"When?" she asked sharply, wishing that being held by him didn't feel so good. "After you've moved into my house?"

"Is that your way of telling me I can live here?"

"No," she retorted. "It's my way of telling you we're going to have to talk about these things before we can even begin to talk about your moving in with me."

Keith tightened his embrace, compelling her body against his. He ran his hands up and down her spine. "We aren't going to talk about any of it tonight."

"What are we going to do?" she asked, her voice muffled by the fabric of his sweater as her lips pressed into his shoulder.

His answer was to slide his hand up to the back of her head and tilt it, to seek her mouth with his. His kiss was tender, slow and poignant. Annie felt sadness in it as well as yearning. She felt Keith's acceptance of the bounds within which they had to function.

They had love, but it was an incomplete love.

Despite its sadness—or maybe because of it—his kiss mesmerized her, aroused her, caused her to ache for him. She would submit to that incomplete love, to accept it as Keith did. But, instead of sweeping her out of the kitchen and down the hall to the bedroom, as Annie had expected he would, Keith drew back and gazed down at her lightly freckled face, at her blue eyes with their shimmer of tears. "Why did Justine come to you?" he asked, shattering the mood his kiss had evoked. "You're the librarian, not her buddy."

"She thinks I'm her buddy," Annie said. At one time, she might have complained about that, but not tonight. Tonight she felt a strong sympathy for the little girl who'd been overlooked while her mother was enduring a marital upheaval.

Keith contemplated Annie's words and shook his head. "She wanted to live here. I think—I think she views you as a mother figure."

"I can't imagine why," Annie argued. "I don't think I've been particularly maternal with her."

Keith continued to study Annie. Again, she saw the flicker of emotion in those profound gray irises, the hint of feelings unspoken but real, burning deep inside him. "You should be a mother, Annie," he whispered. "You were so good at it."

He shut his mouth, stifling himself before more dangerous words escaped. Annie stared at him, astounded. He had never expressed such an opinion before, not even when she had been a mother. Why was he saying it now? And why, why couldn't they keep themselves from trespassing on the issues they wanted so desperately to avoid?

As Keith folded his hand around hers and led her down the hall to her bedroom, Annie knew the subject was closed. They were once again safe from peril, at least temporarily. Their love would stave off those thoughts for now.

Still, she couldn't prevent a few bitter tears from accumulating along the fringe of her eyelashes. She and Keith would love each other tonight, but their love wouldn't be enough. It would never be enough.

Ten

Somewhere around three o'clock, he stopped following the trial and started thinking about Sophie.

Court would be in recess soon enough. Judge Howland was known for his eagerness to get home by dinnertime. One of the reasons the trial was taking so long was that Howland kept gaveling the proceedings to a halt promptly at four-thirty.

As trials went, this one was complicated but not particularly gripping. Keith knew that Steve needed his assistance, and he was doing his best to provide it. But there was a limit to how many statisticians Keith could listen to in testimony before his mind began to wander.

Yesterday, his mind had wandered to the Brenton Motor Inn, to the nondescript room in which he'd stayed the first time he went to Connecticut. The motel's rates were reasonable, and Keith felt confident that he'd have to stay there only about a week before he'd find a suitable residence—if not in Brenton, then in the nearby city of Meriden.

Yet what was the point of that? What did Meriden have that Los Angeles didn't have—other than snow? Keith didn't want to live near Annie; he wanted to live *with* her. If he wasn't going to live with her, he might as well not move to Connecticut at all. The nation was filled with quaint, unpolluted towns in need of lawyers willing to handle local legal tasks at low fees. The only thing Brenton had going for it was Annie.

Keith found himself contemplating the possibility that his whole plan was foolish. Annie loved Keith—at least, she'd certainly seemed to love him enough the Saturday morning they'd spent together in her bed. But when he mentioned his interest in moving in with her, she'd said that he was rushing her.

Rushing her? Hell, they'd rushed each other eight years ago. Barely out of school, drunk on independence and make-believe sophistication, they'd romped off to the hinterlands and played house—and brought a child into the world. *That* was rushing.

But now Keith was older. The years had seasoned him. At long last he was mature enough to know what he wanted, and he was approaching middle age fast enough to know that he didn't have time to waste.

Annie was stalling, though. He'd called her once, about a week after he left Connecticut, and she'd spent most of the call talking about Justine Willis. Justine wasn't such a bad kid, Annie had insisted. Even Justine's mother wasn't so bad. The poor woman was going through hell—and inadvertently dragging her daughter along with her. "Sometimes people go a little crazy when they're sad," Annie had concluded. "That's not such a terrible thing, you know."

As if she were lecturing him, as if she were instructing him. He'd gone plenty crazy after leaving Annie. He didn't need her to explain it to him.

"I mean," she'd continued, "maybe a person earns points for staying cool, but those kinds of points aren't necessarily a measure of human worth."

"Annie, I know that," Keith had snapped. "Why are you coming down on me?"

She'd grown silent, and the call had ended soon afterward. Once he'd hung up, Keith had gone outside for a swim, even though November evenings were a bit chilly for outdoor swimming. He'd swum a mile, then gone upstairs, showered, eaten and climbed into bed. He'd lain awake for hours, churning with anger and frustration. Who the hell was Annie that she felt she had the right to teach him about grief? Who was she to describe the correct way to survive an emotional calamity? Why couldn't she just grow up and accept Keith the way he was?

And why, despite his resentment, did he still want her? Why did even the most disappointing conversation with Annie make him long for her, make him close his eyes and wish she were with him right now, naked, loving him?

He tried not to think so much about Annie, but it was hard. It was especially hard being irritated by her and craving her at the same time. If Keith didn't get his life back on track soon, he'd probably go certifiably insane. Or else he'd run off to the Imperial Valley to harvest tomatoes again.

For a change, however, his mind didn't wander to Annie that afternoon in court. It wandered, instead, to Sophie, the dragon heroine of that children's story Annie liked to tell. He'd heard her tell it twice. The first time was at the department store where he'd ended his long search for her. She'd sat at the center of a swarm of transfixed children, narrating the marvelous fairy tale in her soft, melodious voice, with her hair spilling down her back in a golden cascade and with her eyes as bright and animated as those of her audience. If she'd been a total stranger, Keith would have become instantly infatuated with her.

The second time he'd heard her tell the story was at her house, for Justine Willis. Afterward, unable to smother the thought, Keith had told Annie she'd been a good mother. He'd known that such a remark was out of bounds, but it was the truth.

He should have told her long ago, when the issue of motherhood had been relevant to her life. But he'd told her that Saturday evening, when he'd finally found the courage to say it. They'd returned to her bedroom and made love, and when they were done, Annie had burst into tears. "I'm not ready for this, Keith," she'd sobbed. "I'm not ready for all this."

"What do you think?" Steve whispered as the statistician currently on the stand was dismissed by the judge. "How many more expert witnesses do you think we'll need?"

"You want my honest opinion?" Keith responded softly, dragging his attention back to the trial in progress. He tapped the eraser end of his pencil against the yellow legal pad on the table in front of him and said, "We ought to start something new. The statistics are getting redundant."

"I want to drive home the point that women are scarce in the upper echelons of the company," Steve asserted.

"Sure, drive it home. Don't drive it into the ground."

Steve nodded. "One more statistician, and we'll be done for today. I'll start putting the plaintiffs on the stand tomorrow." He stood and turned to the judge. "Your honor, I'd like to call as my next witness Dr. Harriet Morse, a professor of statistics at U.C.L.A."

Keith sighed. Listening halfheartedly to the new witness as she corroborated everything every other statistician had said on the stand, he checked his wristwatch, studied the judge and tried to predict when the trial would be recessed for the day. At times, he wished he hadn't volunteered to help Steve with this case. The only good thing about it was that as long as he was needed here, he could delay coming to terms with Annie.

Judge Howland called the recess at four-fifteen, a few minutes earlier than Keith had expected. He and Steve gathered their notes, thanked their expert witnesses for their testimony, offered a few words of optimism to the plaintiffs seated in the front-row seats, directly behind the lawyers' table, and then waited their turn to pass through the center aisle leading out of the courtroom.

"I guess you're right," Steve conceded, double-checking the lock on his briefcase. "Enough is enough. We've been spewing statistics at the jury for a week now. We don't want to look like that's all we've got going for us."

"Uh-huh," Keith concurred in a weary grunt. As soon as he crossed the threshold into the bustling corridor, he lifted his hand to his necktie and tugged the knot loose. He wondered if George McKenna wore neckties to work.

The blond woman seated halfway down the corridor on one of the cushioned benches lining the wall caught Keith's eye, and he stumbled a step. It was uncanny how much the woman looked like Annie, with that long flaxen hair and those exquisitely hollow cheeks. Or maybe she only seemed to resemble Annie because lately Keith had been obsessed by thoughts of her.

He quickened his pace to catch up with Steve, who was voicing some ideas about the direction he intended to take when he examined the first of the plaintiffs. Keith's gaze veered toward the woman again, and when her stunning blue eyes met his he knew she was no product of his overwrought imagination. "Annie," he gasped.

"What?" Steve asked.

Keith froze. Oblivious to Steve and to the countless people milling around them in the corridor, he focused solely on the woman coming toward him—the woman who had said that she wasn't ready for him. She was dressed in an attractive flowered skirt and matching sweater, and she carried a large leather purse over her shoulder. Her eyes never strayed from Keith as she neared him.

Puzzled, Steve watched her approach. "Someone you know?" he asked Keith.

Keith barely had the strength to nod. All his energy was concentrated on Annie, on her elegance as she wove through the crowd in her modest high heels, on the dramatic sweep of her hair across her shoulders and upper back. "Hello, Keith," she said with admirable composure.

"What the hell are you doing here?" he blurted out, not at all sure why his soul underwent a sudden surge of joy at seeing her. He was joyful, yes, but also apprehensive, and annoyed. Their common territory was Brenton, Connecticut, not Los Angeles. Los Angeles belonged to Keith. It was his childhood home, his refuge, the place where he lived alone. Annie wasn't supposed to be here.

"I came to see you," she explained, stating the obvious.

"How?" he asked stupidly. "How did you get here?"

"By airplane," she answered, a smile teasing her lips.

Steve cleared his throat. "Is anyone going to introduce me?"

The question cut through the haze fuzzing Keith's brain. "Annie Jameson, Steve Malone," he recited.

Annie presented Steve with her hand, and he shook it. "I'm Keith's ex-wife," she said smoothly.

Keith supposed he had it coming; he'd identified himself as her ex-husband to the owner of the department store where he'd located her. Still, he was surprised by the fact that he wasn't surprised. Annie had worn his ring, and her claim made a certain kind of sense deep inside him. He felt no need to refute it.

"Ex-wife?" Steve exclaimed. "Keith, what have you been hiding from us? And furthermore—" he gave Annie an appreciative inspection "—whatever possessed you to let a lovely woman like this get away?"

"It's a long story," Keith said. Even if it weren't, he'd never share it with Steve. He didn't discuss his personal history with anyone, other than Annie.

He turned to her, still astonished by her presence in the courthouse building. "How did you find me here?" he asked.

"I went to your office," she explained. Her eyes seemed to lose their luster when she added, "I have no idea where you live, Keith."

Fair enough. He'd had no idea where she lived when he embarked on his hunt for her, either, so he'd found her through her job. Now she'd found him through his.

Steve appeared far too interested in their conversation, so Keith took Annie's elbow and ushered her down the corridor to the elevator, Steve walking close behind. Keith tried not to respond to the feel of her arm or the faint scent of her perfume, but it was difficult. It was difficult to resist the urge to bury his lips in the silky blond hair just inches from his chin, to arch his arm around her narrow waist, to close both arms around her and pull her to him and kiss her.

No. They'd had their weekend for that. Two weeks ago— too long ago. They'd attempted to ignore everything else, and it hadn't worked. It hadn't worked at all.

During the elevator ride to the first floor, Keith remained silent, his hand lingering on Annie's elbow. He wondered whether the polite contact between their bodies did as many strange things to Annie's nervous system as it did to his.

"Do you have a car?" he broke in as they made their way through the crowded lobby and then outside.

Annie turned to him. "You mean, did I rent one? No. I took a cab from the airport, and a bus from your office over here."

"A bus? I didn't know L.A. had buses," Steve piped up.

"I think it has two," Keith rejoined. "But Annie's probably the first person who ever used one. My car is parked over there," he said, leading her down the steps to the sidewalk. "I'll see you tomorrow, Steve."

"Right. We'll put some plaintiffs on the stand," Steve called to him before heading down the street in the opposite direction.

Keith led Annie to his car and unlocked the passenger door for her. Once she was settled, he closed her door and strode around to the driver's side. He climbed in next to her, slipped off the jacket of his gray suit, and unfastened his collar button. He stuck the key into the ignition, but he didn't start the engine. Instead, he turned to Annie.

"You aren't happy to see me," she guessed before he could speak.

"I'm not sure how I feel," he confessed. It wasn't a lie, but it wasn't the whole truth, either. He didn't think he was happy—it seemed too uncomplicated an emotion—but he did know that her nearness made his body hum with excitement. Anger and lust were not mutually exclusive.

Annie lowered her eyes to the gear stick separating her seat from his. She pressed her fingertips together, a sign of nervousness. "I had to borrow money from Teri for the airplane ticket," she revealed in a soft voice. "I can't afford a hotel, Keith, I—"

"Don't be silly," he silenced her. "You'll stay with me."

"Are you sure?" She dared to lift her eyes briefly to him, then lowered them again. "After the way I fell apart, the last time you were in Brenton..."

"That was different," Keith said. He wasn't sure why, but he knew that it was. He was as much to blame for what had happened then as Annie was. He shouldn't have brought up the idea of moving in with her. That visit hadn't been an occasion to work things out.

Perhaps this visit was. It had to be. If they couldn't work it out now...

"I have a suitcase," she went on, still addressing the gear stick. "I left it with the receptionist at your office."

"Fine," Keith said, starting the car. At least he had some idea of where to go: first to his office, and then to his apartment. The drive would probably take them an hour, what with the rush-hour traffic beginning to build.

In one hour, they might be able to work everything out. Or they might conclude that they'd never work anything out. With a combination of dread and relief, Keith edged the car out of its parking space.

"How's Justine?" he asked, cruising toward the corner. As soon as he spoke, he winced. Surely he and Annie had more important things to talk about than Justine.

"She isn't whining so much anymore," Annie reported. "Her mother's finally agreed to the divorce. I think Madelyn's devastated, but Justine's bearing up okay."

"I bet all the attention you've been giving her has helped."

"I certainly hope it has," Annie declared firmly, then smiled. "I'd hate to have spent all that time for nothing."

"She's still a pest, huh," Keith deduced, smiling as well.

Annie nodded. "Still a pest. Only now, I understand her a little better."

Annie fell silent, and Keith resisted the temptation to strike up another insignificant conversation. He meditated about what Annie had told him—that she would be staying in his apartment, and that she'd borrowed money from her sister to come here. Teri loathed Keith; she'd done nothing to disguise that fact when Keith had gone to Portland to see her. She blamed him for breaking Annie's heart—and yet she'd lent Annie the money to come to Los Angeles to see him. Maybe she'd hoped that Annie's presence in L.A. would be some kind of torture for Keith.

Maybe it was. It was too early to tell.

"Here's my office," Keith said, pulling into a no-parking zone in front of the skyscraper on Wilshire Boulevard. "Why don't you wait here while I run into the building and get your suitcase? I'll leave the keys in the car, so if a cop comes along you can drive around the block." He could have parked in the underground garage of the building, but if he'd used the garage he couldn't have left Annie alone in that gloomy, spooky area; he would have had to bring her up to the office.

He didn't want her to come upstairs with him. He needed to be alone for a few minutes, to clear his head and figure out what to do. He needed desperately to get away from her.

Keith's abrupt disappearance into the building unnerved her. He had a right to be jumpy, she supposed. She'd been jumpy when he had appeared unexpectedly in Brenton.

She'd found him the way he'd found her, and she'd arrived with the same uncertainties he must have felt when he'd walked in on her story hour at Shandler's Department Store. And, just as he'd had to see her then, she had to see him now.

It was all so clear to her. The more time she spent with Justine and Madelyn Willis, the more Annie began to realize how wrong she'd been—how wrong both she and Keith had been. She'd called Keith at work one time, hoping to explain it to him, but when the secretary had told her he was in court Annie hadn't bothered to leave a message. Some things, she recognized, couldn't be discussed over the telephone.

Teri had been apoplectic when Annie had called and begged her for a loan. "Annie, you know I'd give you whatever you need," Teri had sworn. "Anything at all. I earn twice as much as you do; you know I'll give it to you. But not for *that*. Not so you can see *him*."

"I know you think Keith's the worst thing ever to happen to me," Annie had allowed. "But Teri—it's my life. I love him, and I've got to see him. I've got to make him understand."

"How can you love him? He broke your heart."

"He was able to break my heart because I gave it to him," Annie had responded. "Broken or whole, it still belongs to him. I can't fight it anymore."

Teri had issued a string of curses, but ultimately she'd promised to send Annie the money. Annie was able to pay for the airfare with her November rent money, and she deposited Teri's check in time to keep her rent check from bouncing.

And here she was. For the first time in six years, she was in California. Los Angeles wasn't Orland, but California included both. Annie had met Keith in this state, lived with him here, given birth to Adam and lost him here. There was a time when she'd believed she would never again set foot on California soil for the rest of her life—but she'd come a long way since then.

She spotted Keith amid a throng of business people emerging through the glass doors of the skyscraper. He carried her suitcase, and his expression was unreadable. Annie momentarily closed her eyes and prayed for success. She had to convince Keith that, no matter what she'd told him at her house, no matter how unready she was, she loved him, and their love would enable them to conquer the past. She had to prove it to him. Her emotional survival—and Keith's—depended on it.

Without a word, he tossed her suitcase onto the backseat of the car and slid behind the wheel. He started the engine and merged with the flow of traffic.

"How is the trial going?" Annie asked. It seemed like a safe subject.

Keith shrugged. Annie found herself staring at the rugged breadth of his shoulders beneath the pale blue cotton of his shirt, the strong line of his neck, the rigid angle of his jaw offering a balance to his prominent nose. His opaque gray eyes were riveted to the road.

"Is your side going to win?" she persevered.

"I don't know," he said laconically.

Determined to shake a reaction out of him, Annie asked, "Are you going to make love to me when we get to your home?"

Her bold question had the intended result. Keith turned to gape at her, his gaze remaining on her long enough to cause a car behind him to honk loudly, and Keith's head snapped forward again. A wry smile twisted his mouth. "What would that accomplish?"

His cynical remark didn't bode well. Annie lowered her eyes to her lap again, ran her fingers over her skirt to smooth the fabric across her knees, and sighed. "It would remind us of how much we love each other," she suggested timidly.

"Do we?" Keith shot back. "Is it love? I'm not sure anymore, Annie. The last time I made love to you you burst out crying and told me I was rushing you." He grimaced at the memory. "Do you know how that made me feel?"

"You wouldn't be rushing me now," Annie vowed. "I've finally caught up with you, Keith." Judging from his caustic comments, she suspected that she'd actually moved ahead of him.

"What does that mean?" he asked. "Did you fly all the way out her just to let me know that I'm welcome in your house?"

"No." Annie took a deep breath and forced her eyes to him. "I flew all the way out here to tell you much more than that."

He mulled over her statement, and his smile gradually became more natural. "Something tells me this visit hasn't got the same restrictions as our last visit had."

"I hope not," Annie said, acknowledging to herself that Keith had as much a right as she did to lay down rules. But she didn't want any subject to be off-limits this time.

Now that she'd assured him that he could broach any subject with her, Keith chose to fall silent. He navigated the car carefully through the dense traffic, heading north and east. Annie gazed out the window, trying to imagine how she'd muster the courage to say everything she'd come here to say, trying to imagine what Keith's response would be.

They exited the freeway in Pasadena. Annie mouthed the name silently to herself, forgiving Teri for having confused it with Altadena.

Not far from the freeway, Keith steered into a nondescript complex consisting of four terraced apartment houses surrounding a landscaped patio, at the center of which was a swimming pool. Keith parked in a numbered parking space, climbed out and pulled his jacket and briefcase and Annie's bag from the backseat. Annie let herself out of the car, and Keith locked it.

They strolled up a winding sidewalk to one of the buildings. Keith made no move to take Annie's hand. He held the outer door for her—a gesture of courtesy, nothing more—and then stopped by the mailboxes to pick up his mail before leading her to the elevator.

If he wanted to make love to her—if he loved her—he would have given her some sign of affection. Annie felt her heart sink as she waited with him for the elevator. He was watching her, but she detected no light in his eyes, no warmth in his thin smile.

At last they reached his apartment. It was austerely furnished; the rooms contained only what was necessary. At first Annie assumed that, in preparation for his move, Keith might have begun packing the knicknacks and dust collectors that gave a home its character. But eventually she realized that Keith didn't own any knicknacks and dust collectors. His coffee table held only a professional journal and a popular novel with a bookmark protruding from the pages. The shelves contained the components of a stereo system, a television set and nothing more. The walls were devoid of decoration. The built-in curio nook in the dining room was empty.

Keith's apartment had all the impersonality of his room at the Brenton Motor Inn.

"Why haven't you settled in here?" she asked, unable to suppress her astonishment.

Keith tossed his briefcase and jacket onto an easy chair, then placed Annie's suitcase at the entry to the hallway. "What do you mean, settled in?" he asked, unbuttoning his cuffs and rolling up his sleeves.

"I mean...do you rent this place furnished?" Even the furniture, Annie noted, had a bland look to it.

Keith confirmed her guess with a nod. "It seemed easier than furnishing it myself."

"Yes, but..." She drifted off, surveying the room, crossing over to the window and peering down at the palm lined courtyard below. "You haven't done much to make this apartment your own, have you," she said, turning back to him.

Keith shrugged again. He tugged his tie through the button-down collar of his shirt and tossed it onto the chair. Then he shoved a thick lock of hair off his forehead with his hand. "I guess I never expected to stay here so long," he conceded. "I spent a lot of time moving around before I landed in L.A. And even after four years, I know it's not home."

"Is home Brenton, Connecticut?" Annie asked anxiously.

Keith's long legs carried him across the living room in a few strides and he gazed down at Annie, his body just inches from hers but his hands remaining resolutely at his sides. "Why did you come here, Annie?" he whispered. "Are you going to be able to make it all better for us? Because I'm so tired of hurting, Annie. I'm so tired of it."

She lifted her arms to ring his waist and gave him a gentle hug. "I'm tired of it, too," she murmured, resting her head against his shoulder and willing him to soften to her, to return her embrace. "I came, Keith, because I think I've figured out what went wrong."

"What went wrong was that our baby died," Keith said bluntly.

"That was part of it," Annie admitted, nestling closer to him, longing for the comforting feel of his arms around her. "Keith, I've been watching the Willises these past two weeks, and do you know what went wrong for them? Madelyn was so wrapped up in her own pain, she completely ignored the person who meant the most to her: her own daughter. Madelyn was so busy tending to her own wounds that it never even occurred to her to see how badly hurt Justine was."

Instead of returning her hug, Keith leaned back and stared at her. "What do Justine and her mother have to do with us?"

"Don't you see? That's exactly what we did, Keith. When Adam died, I was so immersed in my pain, I never acknowledged the possibility that you could be in as much pain as me. I kept thinking, you took care of things, you never cried—you couldn't possibly be as badly hurt by it as I was."

"But I *was* hurt—"

"Of course you were, Keith. And so was I. But you saw me meeting with the SIDS support group and thought that I was healing faster than you, that I wasn't grieving so much anymore. Don't you see, Keith?" She wanted to shake him by his shoulders. It was so obvious to her, why wasn't it obvious to him? "Madelyn loves Justine, but she cut her off. She didn't want her daughter to be exposed to her pain, and she concealed it by avoiding Justine. That's what we did, Keith. We burrowed down into ourselves and avoided each other."

Keith continued to study her, dubious. "And now?" he asked quietly, lifting his hand to brush her hair back from her cheek. "Can we change?"

"I think we already have," Annie said.

Her ran his fingers through her hair again, his eyes bearing down on hers. "It still hurts when I think about Adam," he admitted.

"It still hurts me, too. It always will," said Annie. "But . . . but it no longer hurts me to think about you."

His hand came to rest at the side of her head, and his eyes began to glow. Slowly, frustratingly slowly, he dipped his head down and touched his lips to hers. "I am going to make love to you," he said, belatedly answering her question.

"It's not going to accomplish anything," Annie murmured, her lips moving tenderly against his as they shaped each word.

"It's not supposed to accomplish anything," Keith countered. "But it's one way to prove we aren't avoiding each other anymore."

With that, he lifted her into his arms and strode down the hall with her. Entering his bedroom, he deposited her gently at the center of his bed, then sat on the mattress beside her. He pulled off her shoes and tossed them onto the carpeted floor, then located the waistband button of her skirt. In turn, Annie reached up to undo his shirt. As soon as it was open, she slid her hands underneath the crisp cotton to touch his chest.

His breathing became ragged. "I guess we couldn't have avoided this forever," he commented, lifting her hips in order to slide her skirt down her legs. With it came her slip and stockings. Once those garments had joined her shoes on the floor, he glided his hands back up her legs to her panties. He ran his finger along the elastic trim circling her thigh and murmured, "I don't know how I avoided you as long as I did."

"We could have continued avoiding each other," Annie argued, pulling his shirt off his shoulders and down his arms, then drawing her fingers to his belt. "We could have done it forever, Keith, and wound up two bitter, lonely people."

"This way is definitely better," Keith asserted, stripping off her panties and the rest of their clothes, then covering Annie's body with his own. When he ravaged her lips with a penetrating kiss, Annie's tongue met his and her entire body flooded with a hot expectancy.

She stroked his hair, his back, the hard width of his shoulders and the muscular contours of his arms. When her hands reached his, he wove his fingers through hers and pinned her arms to the mattress. Then he kissed her chin, her cheeks, her throat. "You were right to come here," he declared, rising and freeing her hands. He bent to touch one of her breasts with his lips, dropping a teasingly light kiss onto the nipple and sighing with satisfaction as it shrank into a flushed point. He performed the same magic on her other breast, then lifted his head to view her again. "You were right to come after me, Annie."

"You were right to come after me, too," she admitted. Indeed, it had taken much greater bravery on his part to seek her out. He hadn't known whether he'd ever find her, or what she'd be like if he did find her. For Annie, the hardest part of coming to Los Angeles was being able to regain Keith's trust.

"I love you," she whispered, gazing up into his eyes.

"I know," he agreed, sounding not at all smug. "Love was never the problem between us, Annie."

She nodded. Despite the stimulating closeness of their bodies, the weight of his hips against hers, she saw nothing strange in having this solemn conversation—in sharing their most intimate thoughts before they allowed their bodies further intimacy.

They had never stopped loving each other; she agreed with Keith about that. "I envied your strength, Keith. I think that was what I resented."

"And I resented yours," Keith said, smiling slightly at the irony of it. "I guess neither of us was all that strong."

"We're much stronger together," Annie remarked.

Keith's smile expanded, and his body responded to her comment by uniting with hers with a deep surge. "Oh, yes, Annie," he groaned, running his hands down her sides to her hips, holding her to him. "Much, much stronger."

His voice dissolved into a rumbling sigh as he drew her legs up and around him, as he kissed her. His body surged again, again, driving deeper into her, stroking her with his fierce thrusts, reaching for her essence.

Closing her eyes, Annie let her thoughts travel down to the place where his body and hers were joined. When Keith had visited her in Connecticut, their lovemaking had seemed like something new to her because she'd lived so long without anything like it, without love and the closeness of a man. This time, Keith's lovemaking again seemed novel—gloriously unfamiliar—because now, Annie was willing to accept the many things that bound them together: not just desire, not just love, but the yearning for the strength they found only in each other's arms.

She felt strong now, stronger than she'd ever felt before. She felt strong enough to give herself to Keith, to the love burning between them, building, compelling them upward to a delirious peak. Sensation exploded around Annie, igniting a dark throbbing within her body and her soul until she felt limp and drained and utterly satisfied. Keith followed close behind her, his body fusing to hers in a final, conquering motion.

"Oh, Annie, Annie..." His breath was too shallow to carry his voice, and her name emerged from his lips in a harsh gasp. He closed his arms tightly around her, rolled onto his side, and shut his eyes.

Annie ran her index finger along the edge of his chin and up to his mouth. In spite of his blissful exhaustion, he found the energy to part his lips and catch her fingertip between his

teeth. His eyes fluttered open and he grinned. "I was thinking about Sophie today," he confessed, his voice still un-
even.

"Sophie? The dragon?" Mirroring his smile, Annie nestled closer to him, sliding one of her legs between his and
looping her arm around his waist. She trailed her fingers
over the smooth skin on his back and he sighed content-
edly. "What about Sophie?" she asked before he could melt
fully into her gentle massage.

"Just what a nice story it is. And how nice you sound
telling it." He leaned toward her and kissed her, then settled into the pillow and smiled again, a wistful, introspec-
tive smile. "The smoke can be scary, Annie, but it's worth
overcoming your fear so you can see the rainbow."

"Yes." She shifted her head to share the pillow with him,
and her smile faded. "Keith..." She took a deep breath,
suddenly uncertain, afraid that what she had to say might
not be so easy to accept. "Keith, I wasn't protected. Just
now, when we—"

He brushed his fingers over her mouth to silence her.
When he was sure she wouldn't speak, he pulled his hand
away, then used it to capture hers. He raised it to his mouth
and kissed her palm. "I didn't think you were," he admitted. "And I don't... I don't really mind. Do you?"

Stunned, Annie stared at him. The setting sun slanted
through the window to cast long purple shadows across the
bed, but even in shadow she could see his face. His gray eyes
were clear, his smile relaxed and confident, his dimples fully
displayed. "Aren't you afraid?" I mean, what you said
about your genes and all—"

"Yes," he answered, but his smile didn't falter. "I'm
afraid. But maybe there'll be a rainbow this time." He
grazed her mouth with his once more. "Let's have a baby,
Annie."

"It may be a little late for that suggestion," she said,
surprised at how much the idea thrilled her. She wanted another baby. She didn't mind befriending Justine Willis, but

she wanted a child of her own. A healthy child, as strong as the parents who created it.

"I still have the ring you gave me," he confessed. "Do you still have mine?"

"Yes," she said, amazed that he'd kept the ring. Keith had never been as sentimental as she—and besides, he'd never even worn it when they were together.

As if he could read her mind, he said, "I'll wear it this time. I promise." He kissed her again. "And this time, we'll get married."

"You want the piece of paper?" Annie asked. Her tone was joking, but the emotion underlying it was earnest.

"I'm a lawyer," he reminded her. "I know how important those pieces of paper can be." He closed his arms around her, urging her head away from the pillow and onto his shoulder. "A marriage isn't about a piece of paper, Annie. It's about a structure, a shared strength. Something to hold us together when we lose some of our individual strength."

"If that's your definition of marriage," Annie murmured, "my answer is yes. But," she added, "I hope nothing ever happens to make us lose our strength."

"It will," Keith predicted, sounding not pessimistic but matter-of-fact. "We'll face our share of heartaches, Annie. 'Happily ever after' is for storybooks, not real life. But we will be happy, and when times get rough we'll face the problems together and help each other through."

That sounded wonderful to Annie. She cuddled close to him, certain that as long as they stayed together, as long as they tapped into their shared strength and love, they could face anything. And certain that, no matter what Keith thought, there could be a "happily ever after" in real life—as long as she and Keith didn't lose sight of the rainbow through the smoke.

* * * * *

Silhouette Intimate Moments

Rx: One Dose of

DODD MEMORIAL HOSPITAL

In sickness and in health the employees of Dodd Memorial Hospital stick together, sharing triumphs and defeats, and sometimes their hearts as well. Revisit these special people this month in the newest book in Lucy Hamilton's Dodd Memorial Hospital Trilogy, *After Midnight*—IM #237, the time when romance begins.

Thea Stevens knew there was no room for a man in her life—she had a young daughter to care for and a demanding new job as the hospital's media coordinator. But then Luke Adams walked through the door, and everything changed. She had never met a man like him before—handsome enough to be the movie star he was, yet thoughtful, considerate and absolutely determined to get the one thing he wanted—Thea.

Finish the trilogy in July with *Heartbeats*—IM #245.

Silhouette Desire
COMING NEXT MONTH

#427 ALONG CAME JONES—Dixie Browning
Tallulah Lavender was a pillar of society. Could she throw over a lifetime of dedication to others for a tall, tough rock-slide of a man? She hesitated . . . then along came Jones!

#428 HE LOVES ME, HE LOVES ME NOT—Katherine Granger
Her book was number one, but Delta Daniels nibbled while she worked—the bestselling diet guru was as fat as a blimp! Enter fitness instructor Kyle Frederick, who aroused other, more compelling appetites. . . .

#429 FORCE OF HABIT—Jacquelyn Lennox
That unprincipled man! Health editor Tara Ross refused to let herself fall for sexy Ethan Boone of Logan Tobacco. Still, she couldn't ignore the spark of passion between them.

#430 TO TAME THE WIND—Sara Chance
Jade Hendricks was as wild and elusive as the animals Russ Blackwell trained. Was his love strong enough to tame her restless heart and set her spirit free?

#431 CAN'T SAY NO—Sherryl Woods
Blake Marshall didn't give Audrey Nelson a chance to say no when he literally swept her off her feet and into his balloon. But would she say yes to love?

#432 MOON OF THE RAVEN—Joyce Thies
The first of three *Tales of the Rising Moon*. One look at ranch foreman Conlan Fox, and Kerry Armstrong knew she'd do anything to win the man of her dreams.

AVAILABLE NOW: